FAMINE IN FRENCH VANILLA

More books by Suzan Harden
(Each series is in suggested reading order)

Bloodlines
Blood Magick
Zombie Love
Zombie Confidential
Zombie Wedding
Amish, Vamps & Thieves
Blood Sacrifice
Love, War & a Bulldog
Zombie Goddess
Ravaged
Sacrificed
Reality Bites
Ghouls in the Grocery Store
Resurrected
Bloodlines Shorts Anthology
Bloodlines: The First Boxed Set

Seasons of Magick
Spring
Summer
Autumn
Winter
The Seasons of Magick Anthology

Justice
Sword and Sorceress 28 ("Justice")
Sword and Sorceress 30 ("Diplomacy in the Dark")
Justice: The Beginning
A Question of Balance
A Modicum of Truth
A Matter of Death
A Touch of Mother
A Twist of Love
A Virtue of Child
A Hand of Father
A Measure of Knowledge
A Hint of Thief

The Justice Thalia Stories
Snowfall
Murder Most Fowl
The Sweetest Poison
A Granddaughter of Mine

Tales of the Twelve
The Trickster Priestess and the Demon

888-555-HERO
Hero De Facto
Hero Ad Hoc
Hero De Novo
A Very Hero Christmas
Hero De Jure
Hero In Camera
Hero Amicus Curiae
A Very Hero Wedding
A Very Hero New Year
Hero Ad Litem
Queer Eye for the Super Guy

Solar System Services, Inc.
Alone Is Not Lonely

Millersburg Magick Mysteries
Spells and Sleuths
Fae and Felonies
Magick and Murder

Soccer Moms of the Apocalypse
Pestilence in Pumpkin Spice
Famine In French Vanilla
War in White Chocolate
Death in Double Mocha

Miscellaneous
Sword and Sorceress 31 ("Pig-Headed")
Sword and Sorceress 32 ("Unexpected")
Practical Witches
Revenge Served Hot
The Yule Switch
Chocolate for Dinner
Silver Shoes and Pigs' Ears

For updates, news, and giveaways, join Suzan's mailing list or visit her website at www.suzanharden.com. You can also check her out on Twitter or Facebook.

Famine in French Vanilla

SUZAN HARDEN

This is a work of fiction. All characters, organizations and events in this story are products of the author's imagination and are not to be construed as real. Any resemblance to persons, living or dead, is entirely coincidental.

FAMINE IN FRENCH VANILLA
(Soccer Moms of the Apocalypse #2)

ISBN-13 - 978-1-64918-016-2

Published by Angry Sheep Publishing
Findlay, Ohio

Interior Design by JW Manus
Cover Design by For the Muse Designs

*To Karen, who thought the idea of the
Soccer Moms of the Apocalypse was as funny as I did*

Chapter 1

The buzzing of her phone drew Francine Coy-Astin out of a deep sleep. The barest light passed through the sheer white drapes of her bedroom. God help her, she hated autumn. The shorter days meant she wasn't getting enough sunlight, which in turn meant a lack of vitamin D and a corresponding lack of energy.

Whoever was calling her would leave a message. She snuggled deeper into the lavender-scented pillows and comforter and reached for Neal, but her body only met cooler sheets. That's right. Her husband left early this morning for his monthly meeting with the sales team. Bless him, he'd managed to shower and dress without waking her.

Nor did their daughter Brittany have school today due to in-service training and parent conferences. Francine made a point of setting up all her appointments with Brittany's teachers on Thursday so they could have this one Friday to sleep in a little.

The buzzing of the phone stopped, only to start again. Francine groaned and rolled over to reach for the device. If it was Mom calling to complain about the "hooligans" next door at their Florida condominium again, Francine would turn off the damn phone.

Instead, the caller ID said "Penny".

That jerked Francine out of her semi-conscious state. Penny knew better than to call this early in the morning, which meant it was something she couldn't handle as Pestilence. Francine sat up and tapped the answer icon. "What's wrong?"

"My mother-in-law just showed up on my doorstep." Penny sounded like she was about to hyperventilate.

"Girl, you had a nightmare," Francine said soothingly. When the hell had she switched roles with Penny? She was Miz Practical, not Francine. "Your mother-in-law passed away. She's in her grave in Oakfield Cemetery—"

"No, she's not," Penny hissed. "She's sitting in my living room. Edward and Justine are eating breakfast in the kitchen, and they're going to discover Laura any moment."

"That can't be." Despite all the weirdness with their new roles and demons over the last couple of weeks, this went one step too far. "She died. We went to her funeral—"

"Francine, what's the fifth seal of Revelations?" Penny's voice had an edge of hysteria.

The rising of the dead from their graves. That rhetorical question swept away the last sleep cobwebs. "Shit," Francine muttered. "Let me get dressed, and I'll be right over."

After warning Brittany to stay inside and keep the doors locked until Francine returned, she headed for the Hudsons' house fifteen minutes later. She wasn't about to put her own daughter in danger if Penny's zombie mother-in-law was actually inside the Hudsons house.

Stopped at a traffic light after a side trip to The Bake Shoppe's drive-thru, Francine's favorite local radio station broke for news. She didn't pay attention until the announcer chuckled. "On a local note, police arrested a man at the Oakfield Court House. He claimed he was one of our city's founders, Jebediah Hauser, and demanded that people get off his property. My assistant Kat did a little digging on this one, and Hauser did in fact own the land where the courthouse sits. His widow sold the property to Ebenezer Dorchester in 1822."

Francine bit her lower lip. She didn't find mental illness funny at all.

She hoped the man got the care he needed. But what if Penny was right, and the Fifth Seal had broken? What if the man the police arrested was the real Jebediah Hauser risen from the dead?

The light turned green, and Francine pressed the accelerator. Her skin tingled, an indication her Horseman Famine wanted to rear her ugly head. She tried to focus on the two boxes of crème-filled Long Johns sitting in the passenger seat to keep her alter ego in check. The other girls had to concentrate to bring forth their Horsemen personas, or rather their Soccer Moms of the Apocalypse as Wila liked to call them. Francine had the opposite problem. She had to concentrate to keep hers in check.

As she found out the hard way when she accidentally started a riot at the Oakfield Buffet one afternoon with her supernatural hunger.

Francine pulled next to the curb in front of Penny's house. The construction workers who replaced the splintered front door and its frame had done an excellent job. They just needed to be painted to match the shutters and trim, and no one would know anything had happened.

Except she did. She'd smacked Penny's husband Gene with her scales right through the old door. The only reason he was still alive was thanks to the strength of the bastard demon who had possessed him. But the demon had been about to stab Penny, so Francine didn't have much of a choice.

She cut the engine of her minivan before she slung her tote over her shoulder, grabbed one box of the pastries, and retrieved a wad of napkins from the glove box. Her seat vibrated, an indication Sable sensed something out of the ordinary. If Penny really did have her mother-in-law inside, Sable undoubtedly picked up on the dead woman's presence.

"You need to stay here and behave yourself." Francine patted the dashboard. "Penny would know if it was a demon."

She exited her vehicle/horse and jogged up the couple of steps to Penny's front porch. The wind carried that first sharp hint of winter and seemed determined to pull off the remaining red leaves from the oak trees along the street. Not bothering to ring the doorbell, she pressed the latch of the new front door and shoved it open.

The door to the formal living room was closed. Penny only closed off the living room when Gene had his medical colleagues over for one of their get-togethers. Muddy footprints caked the entryway mat, and more dirt was scattered on the hardwood floor in a direct path to the living room.

Francine closed the front door, unsure of how to proceed. If she knocked, she'd alert Edward and Justine that something was going on. She pulled her phone out of its slot on her tote, turned off the sound on the device, and texted Penny.

I'm right outside the living room door. Safe to come in?

A second later, Francine's phone vibrated with Penny's reply.

Yes

Francine sucked in a deep breath, pushed down on the latch, and opened the door. A woman with disheveled brunette hair and wearing a very filthy pale blue linen spring suit sat on the couch next to Penny. She resembled Penny's mother-in-law if you erased twenty or thirty years and the ravages of her ovarian cancer. Both women clutched mugs of coffee, Penny's favorite pumpkin spice and peppermint for the other woman from the odors.

Penny's shoulders relaxed a bit at Francine's entrance. "Thank you for coming over."

The other woman looked at Francine and smiled. "Hello, Francine." She may have needed a shower and clean clothes, but with that pleasant expression, she definitely looked just like Penny's late mother-in-law Laura Hudson.

Francine held up her box. "Anyone want a Long John?"

Chapter 2

Francine set the box of crème-filled doughnuts and napkins on the coffee table and dropped her tote on the floor before she stripped off her coat and tossed it on one of the blue-upholstered Queen Anne chairs opposite of the couch. She plopped on the other chair and regarded Penny. Her friend looked like she was about to have a breakdown from the way her hands shook despite her tight grip on her coffee mug.

"How are you keeping Edward and Justine out?" Francine asked.

"I told them you were already here, and we needed some privacy to talk about Soccer Mom stuff," Penny said.

"Are Justine and Brittany still playing soccer?" Laura brightened. "That's cool. There were so many stupid restrictions on girls in sports when I was their age."

"Yes, they are, and they're loving it." Francine opened the box. "I hope you don't mind, but I haven't had breakfast yet." She reached for a doughnut. "And I'm starving."

"Crap," Penny murmured. "You should have taken the time to eat." She jumped up from the couch. "I can warm up last night's chicken and rice casserole. Or would you prefer scrambled eggs and bacon?"

Francine held up a hand. "I'm good. I've got an extra box of Long Johns in my minivan. Just in case."

Penny slowly sat back down though she perched on the edge of the couch, probably hoping for another reason to escape from the living room.

Francine held out the box to Laura. "Want one?"

"Those look so good." Laura reached out, then jerked back her hand. "Oh, my god. My hands are filthy. I should wash up—"

"No need to leave." Francine set the box back on the coffee table and her maple Long John on a napkin before she fished the canister of wet wipes out of her tote. "Clean your hands and face. These are organic with all natural cleansers." When Laura took the canister, Francine pulled out a plastic zippered bag from her tote's side pocket.

"Are you sure you're not one of Ed's kids from another woman?" Laura said.

Francine shot a look at Penny.

"She's joking," Penny said. "I think."

"Of course, I'm joking." Laura looked at Penny like she'd grown a second head.

Once Laura cleaned her hands and face, she looked . . . alive, and much younger than Francine remembered from the funeral. She held open the plastic bag for Laura to deposit the used wipes. Her skin felt warm when their fingers brushed.

"I don't understand why I can't see my own husband if he's here." Laura selected a chocolate Long John and took a bite. She chewed normally and swallowed her mouthful.

Once again, Francine exchanged a look with Penny. "We have to tell her the truth."

"Oh, my god." Penny's head dropped into her palms. "Edward, Gene, and Theo are going to freak. And Justine's been through enough."

Laura finished her Long John, took a napkin, and dabbed the chocolate frosting and crème filling from the corners of her mouth. She gave Penny a measured look. "I already know someone else is living in my house. You'd better start from the top and explain everything, young lady, before I make a scene. Then everybody will know I'm here."

Penny seemed frozen in place. The last thing they needed was for her mother-in-law to make good on her threat.

Francine cleared her throat. "What's the last thing you remember, Laura?"

She blinked, then frowned. "That's odd. I-I was in a hospital I think." She looked at Penny again. "Did I have a stroke?"

Penny shook her head. "Do you remember being diagnosed with cancer?"

"I was?" Laura's eyes widened. "I remember Justine having leukemia in first grade, but I don't . . ." Worry creased her forehead.

"You had ovarian cancer," Francine said gently.

"B-but I always had my check-ups," Laura protested.

Francine glanced at Penny, but after the last three weeks, her practical friend had hit the proverbial wall. Francine cleared her throat.

"You had a very aggressive form," she said gently. "The hospital you remember is probably the hospice you had to go to when the tumors in your brain made you unable to perform basic tasks."

"We kept you at home as long as possible, Laura," Penny blurted. "But you needed around the clock care. It was killing Edward. I'm the one who pressed the hospice issue, so please don't blame Edward, Gene, or Theo."

"I died," Laura said. Penny couldn't meet her mother-in-law's gaze. Laura turn to Francine. "Didn't I?"

"Yes," Francine answered.

"I don't understand." Laura frowned. "I mean I believe in God . . ."

"The Four Horsemen manifested on Earth three weeks ago." Francine sympathized with Laura. Wila, Dani, Penny, and she had nearly a month to get used to the idea. They were dumping a hell of a lot on Laura in only five minutes. "We think the fifth seal of the Apocalypse has been broken, and the dead are rising."

"I need another Long John to deal with this." Laura selected a maple one this time.

"Where's Gene if only Edward and Justine are here?" Francine asked.

"He's at Saint Michael's talking with Deke, ur, I mean, Father McAvoy."

Tears welled in Penny's eyes. She was trying so hard to be the strong one. It was going to break her if she didn't let herself process all the stuff that had happened to them.

Laura swallowed her bite of doughnut. "Are you talking about Father Deacon McAvoy?"

"Yes," Francine said.

"Edward and I used to know him years ago. Last I heard, he was . . ." Laura exhaled gustily. "How long ago did I pass away?"

"It was two years in June," Penny said.

"What year is it?" Laura asked.

Francine told her, and Laura nodded.

"All right, so Deacon was supposed to be transferred to Saint James in Chicago four years ago." Laura pursed her lips. "I don't like the fact the last year and a half of my life memories were taken from me."

"It may be that Heaven excised those memories to make it easier on you," Francine suggested. "You were in a terrible amount of pain during that period."

"That makes sense." Laura sagged against the back of the couch. "So, did Edward sell the house after I died?"

Once again, Penny couldn't meet her mother-in-law's eyes.

"Yes," Francine said softly. "He couldn't handle you not being there with him, and he started to have his own health issues. Gene insisted he move into the downstairs bedroom suite here."

"And now, I'm back from the dead." Laura shook her head. "I can't even imagine how this will affect him and the boys."

The door between Penny's living room and her family room burst open. "Mom! Wila says you're not answering your cell phone. She's calling—" Justine stared at Laura. The girl's face turned sheet white, which only emphasized her red curls.

"Grandma?"

Chapter 3

"Justine, what does Wila need?" Francine asked.

Instead of answering, the girl threw herself into Laura's arms, regardless of the grave dirt covering her grandmother.

"Penny!" Edward bellowed.

Francine jumped to her feet. "I'll deal with him and Wila while you take care of Justine and Laura."

The last thing they needed was Edward to have a heart attack or stroke from having his dead wife in the house. Francine strode out of the living room's second entrance from the family room and shut the door behind her. She was supremely glad her parents and Neal's were all alive and living happily in Florida. She couldn't imagine how she would deal with a dead parent showing up on her front porch.

Francine charged into the Hudsons kitchen to find Edward on his cell phone. "Give it to me." She held out her hand.

Surprisingly, he complied without complaining. When she lifted the phone to her ear, it sounded like Wila was in a vehicle.

"It's Francine," she said. "What's going on?"

"I think the Fifth Seal broke," Wila snapped. "I'm on a call—"

Francine rubbed her forehead. "Please tell me you're not calling and driving your rig at the same time."

"It's on speaker, bitch." Wila was silent for a moment before she said, "I'm sorry. I'm freaking out here."

"Just tell me what happened." Francine looked up. Edward was paying close attention to her conversation. Too close. She needed to be careful how she worded things with Wila.

"Brian and I were sent on a 9-1-1 call this morning," she said. "The husband called it in. The wife fainted and hit her head. They're both in the back right now with Brian."

"And?" Francine prompted.

"We had a call to the same address last year," Wila bit out. "The husband had a cardiac event. He was DOA."

Francine shuddered. "Didn't Brian notice it was the same person?"

"He's talked himself into thinking this guy is the deceased's brother," Wila said. "For now anyway. Is Penny okay?"

"No, she's not." Francine sighed. "The last three weeks have cracked her mental health, too, not just Gene's."

A concerned look crossed Edward's face. Crap, that was the wrong thing to say.

"I'm dealing with a similar situation here," Francine continued. "Can you call Dani for backup? I don't know how long Penny will need me to stay here."

Edward shuffled to the coffee pot and refilled his cup before he tottered out of the kitchen. Francine sagged in relief. At least, he wasn't staring at her anymore as he tried to eavesdrop on her conversation with Wila.

"I'm finally alone, so listen fast," Francine murmured. "Penny's mother-in-law showed up here first thing this morning."

"What?" Wila shouted. "She—we were at the damn funeral!"

Francine winced and held the receiver away from her ear. "I know. That's why I have my hands full here."

"Grandpa, no!" Justine shrieked. It was followed by a female scream that was abruptly cut off.

"I gotta go," Francine said. "Call you when I can." She ended the call, set Edward's phone on the table, and raced for the living room.

Only to find Penny and Justine desperately trying to pull Edward off

Laura. He wasn't someone Francine thought of as a violent person, but the revelation he used to be a demon hunter for the Vatican showed how little she knew about Penny's father-in-law, much less anyone else.

"Let her go, Edward!" Francine snapped.

When he didn't, she stopped keeping Famine in check. Her jeans and favorite Halloween sweater melded into her black robes. The odd feeling of her skin tightening flowed over her body.

Penny and Justine backed out of the way as Francine strode over to the couch. She grabbed hold of his collar and belt and yanked him off Laura. Edward flailed. His kick sent the box of Long Johns flying through the air. The box hit the top shelf of the bookcase where Gene kept his collection of antique volumes. The white cardboard tumbled down, depositing frosting, crème, and pastry bits on the contents of every single shelf until the last of the doughnuts splatted all over Penny's brand new cream-colored plush carpet.

A weird gurgling sound came from Laura.

Justine rushed over to the couch. "Are you okay, Grandma?"

"Goddammit, Francine!" Edward shouted. "Put me down! We have to kill it!"

"Listen to me, Edward Hudson," Francine growled. "Think about it. Demons can't possess the dead. That is not a demon!"

His struggles slowed. "But-but—"

"She's right, Edward," Penny said. "If the first four Seals have broken, it makes sense the Fifth Seal would break." She looked at Laura. "It seems sooner rather than later."

On the other hand, Laura stared at Francine, shock muting her despite Justine's repeated questions about her status.

Edward stopped struggling. "Put your hair back on, Francine. I won't fight you anymore."

She set the elderly man upright. Obviously, he still wasn't sure about having his late wife sitting on the living room couch, but he didn't make a move towards Laura.

Francine took a deep breath and shoved her obscene hunger back into its hole. Her black robes faded back into her jeans and black sweater with the jack o'lantern family.

"What are you?" Laura stammered.

"I wasn't joking when I said the Four Horsemen manifested three weeks ago," Francine said. "As you could probably tell from my appearance a moment ago, I'm Famine."

She reached into her right jeans pocket and dug out her keys. "Justine, since your grandfather ruined this box of doughnuts with his homicidal tendencies, would you please grab the extra box sitting in my front seat?"

"Absolutely!" The girl grinned.

Francine tossed her keys to Justine, and the girl ran out of the living room.

"Edward, you are going to clean up the mess you made." Francine waited for him to argue. He did shoot a pleading expression at Penny.

"Uh-uh." His daughter-in-law shook her head. "You made the mess. You clean it up. And you can explain the damage to Gene's books to him."

"Francine's the one who threw a demon through your front door!" he protested. "And I paid for that."

"The girls are right. Clean it up, Ed," Laura snapped.

"All right," he grumbled before he shuffled out of the living room.

"I'm sorry for the way I acted toward you, Francine," Laura said. "Or should I call you Famine?"

"I'm still the Francine you knew." She smiled.

Laura turned to her daughter-in-law. "Penny, would you mind if I use your shower and borrow something to wear?" She brushed at the dirt on her left sleeve. "It seems digging my way out of my grave left my clothing rather filthy."

"Of course." Penny started to leave but stopped and looked over her shoulder at Francine. "Is Wila okay?"

"For now." Francine shooed Penny toward the door closest to their staircase. "Go take care of Laura and I'll tell you the rest when you come back down."

"I got the doughnuts," Justine warbled from the front door.

"To the kitchen with those before there's more chocolate stains on my new carpet," Penny ordered from the landing.

Francine chuckled to herself as she headed to the kitchen, too. All her friends claimed she was the stuck-up one when it came to how her house looked. But she wasn't cutting her chairs in half with a flaming sword or smearing Long Johns all over a priceless book collection and brand-new wall-to-wall carpet.

Chapter 4

Francine entered Penny's kitchen to find Justine eating a chocolate-frosted doughnut.

"Thanks for bringing these," the girl said around a mouthful of pastry.

"You're welcome." Francine smiled. "Do you have any milk to go with them?"

Justine swallowed before she said, "There is some, but it may be a little iffy. With all the trouble between Mom, Dad, and that Rimmon guy—" Frown lines ran between her eyes, and Francine's heart went out to the girl.

Justine licked her lips. "Is he really dead? He won't make Dad do bad stuff again?" Her voice ended on a wobble that indicated she was trying very hard not to cry.

"Rimmon's dead," Francine said. "You don't have to worry about him ever again."

"Grandma was dead." Justine's lower lip trembled. "He might come back, too."

"Oh, sweetie." Francine pulled the girl into a tight hug. "Trust me. He is never coming back. According to my research, only the good people will be brought back. Like your grandmother."

"Can Brittany come over? I'm a-a l-little scared."

Francine smoothed Justine's wayward curls back from her face. "Why don't you video chat with her? Your mom and I need to talk. Would you like to spend the night at our house again?"

Justine shrugged. "I don't know. I-I want to stay here with Grandma. I miss her so much, but—"

"I'm a little weirded out about this whole situation, too." Francine smiled. "Why don't you grab another doughnut and go talk to Brittany? Then we'll make some decisions after your mom and I talk."

Justine nodded before she retrieved a clean plate for the remaining half of the Long John she'd been munching on and selected another chocolate one. She disappeared into the family room.

Ah, to be twelve and able to eat everything again.

Except Francine could eat everything again, but it came at a price. Accepting the role of Famine and battling demons hadn't helped to quell her insane hunger. She ate more in one day than her family ate in an entire month.

Unless she unleashed her hunger on the public. The one time she accidentally had, the police needed riot gear and tear gas to get the restaurant patrons in check.

Francine looked around the Hudsons kitchen. Dirty plates and silverware still sat on the table, which showed how fast things had gone crazy this morning.

Her stomach rumbled. Loudly. She needed to take care of that first. When she retrieved the milk jug from the refrigerator and unscrewed the cap, the slight strawberry-like scent milk had right before it totally soured hit her nose.

Well, she'd take care of it for Penny. If she needed to stay and keep an eye on Penny's in-laws while Penny made a grocery run, she would. And later this weekend, she'd make up for the ruined lunch and shopping trip she'd planned with Brittany. Their friends needed them right now.

Francine cleared the dirty dishes from the table and wiped it down before she sat down with the quarter-filled gallon jug of milk and started eating doughnuts. Unfortunately, every time Famine manifested, she left Francine starving.

Literally.

She was washing down her third Long John with the almost bad milk when Penny walked into the kitchen. She stopped and stared at Francine before she crossed her arms and said, "I knew one box of doughnuts wouldn't be enough for you, but drinking straight out of the jug? That's so not like you, Miss Prim-and-Proper."

Francine lowered the milk and licked her lips. "It's about to go bad. You don't want Justine or Edward to drink this. On the other hand, I will take calories in whatever form they come these days." She burped before she added, "What can I do to help? Besides the dishes once Laura's out of the shower."

Penny flopped onto the chair next to Francine. "I thought everything would get better after Wednesday. I had one day of normalcy. Ugh!" She scrubbed at her face. "Let me guess. Wila called because she ran into a dead person."

Francine nodded. "She and Brian answered a call this morning to the same house where the husband was DOA a year ago. Reading between the lines of what she could tell me, the husband crawled out of his grave and went home, too. The wife fainted and hit her head on the way down. The husband called 9-1-1."

"What about Brian?"

Francine snorted. "He's convinced himself the man who called in is the twin brother of the guy who died."

Penny swore under her breath. "We need to warn Dani."

Horror rippled through Francine. "Oh, god, I wasn't thinking. She and Mark are living in the same house they had when Heath died, isn't she?"

"Yeah." Penny fished her phone out of her front jeans pocket. She tapped the screen before she set the phone between her and Francine on the table. The phone rang once. Twice.

"Hernandez Insurance Agency. Dani speaking. How may I help you?"

"Hey, girl. It's Penny and Francine. Got a minute for some Soccer Mom issues?"

"Not really," Dani grumbled. "But just a sec." Something squeaked before there was carpet shuffling. With the second squeak, Dani said, "Sorry, I needed to make sure I had a little privacy. What happened? Is Pence there to arrest you?"

The police officer was absolutely sure there was something squirrely about Penny, especially after two of the people the demons had possessed were found dead.

Francine bit the side of her cheek to keep from laughing at Penny's sour expression.

"Believe me, I wish it were that easy." Penny sighed wearily. "The Fifth Seal has broken."

"But the Fifth Seal is—ohmigod! We have zombies running around Oakfield?"

"Penny's mother-in-law showed up at her front door this morning," Francine said. "And Wila responded to an EMT call that was made by a guy she and Brian pronounced DOA last year."

"Please tell me this is a practical joke." A sound suspiciously like a sob came through the receiver. "Please, please, please."

"My dead mother-in-law is washing off grave dirt in my shower right now," Penny snapped. "We are not joking."

"Where's Mark?" Francine asked.

"Since there's no school today, he and Derek are at my-my—ohmigod, I can't breathe." Dani was obviously hyperventilating.

"Dani, listen to me," Francine said gently. "Call Mark, and tell him I'm going to your house to pick up him and Derek. I'll call Wila, and let her know what's going on. Then I'll swing by to collect Brittany and bring lunch over to Penny's. Can you take the rest of the day off?"

"Y-y-yeah." A paper bag crinkled through the phone speaker. "I'll tell Marty I have cramps. Th-that works every time with him."

Thank goodness, Dani worked for her brother. Francine couldn't imagine finding excuses to leave her job every time a Soccer Mom emergency came up.

"Hang in there, sweetie," Francine said. "I'll see you when you get here."

"O-okay." Dani sniffed. "I'll see you later."

The phone call ended, and Penny grabbed Francine's hands. "You cannot leave me alone here. Gene will be home at any moment."

"Listen to me, Penny," Francine said softly. "You heard Dani. Imagine how Mark is going to react if Heath shows up at the Elante residence. Why do you think Dani was hyperventilating?"

Penny released Francine's hand and place her own palms over her mouth. She finally lowered her hands. "Can I please trade jobs with you?"

"If Gene tries to hurt Laura or worse, you go Pestilence on his ass," Francine said. "I'll grab my coat. I should be back within an hour. You're the strong one, Penny. You can handle this."

"I really wish you three would stop saying that," Penny grumbled.

Francine gave Penny a quick hug. "I'll be fast I promise."

When Francine entered the living room, Edward was still meticulously wiping sugary gunk from Gene's book collection. He gave her the side-eye as she retrieved her coat and put it on. She grabbed her tote and turned to go when he said, "Are you sure that woman is Laura?"

She pivoted to look at him. "Why? Think she'll interfere with your multitude of girlfriends?"

"Multitude?" He glared at her.

"Edward, I know about you and Deborah Gibson," she hissed.

An alarmed expression crossed his face. "Penny told you?"

Francine rubbed her forehead. "Shit. Does she really know?"

"If she didn't tell you, how do you know?" he asked.

"Deborah was boasting about it at the First Methodist pancake supper last winter." Francine shook her head. "She thought she'd become the new Mrs. Hudson."

Edward pursed his mouth. "You can berate me all you want, but please, don't hurt Laura."

"I have no intention of ruining her life—" She couldn't help a little burble of laughter from erupting. "—or her death. Clean up that mess before I get back with lunch."

He reddened. "I was changing diapers before you were born."

"And I'm sure you were smearing the contents of your diapie on walls long before you smeared perfectly good Long Johns all over your son's books." Francine shot him a cocky smile. "See you in a bit."

She gritted her teeth as she charged out Penny's new front door and strode to her minivan. If Neal's dad were half as obnoxious as Edward Hudson, she would have killed him years ago.

Chapter 5

After considering her route through town between Penny's and Dani's houses, Francine called Brittany and told her to be ready when the minivan pulled into the driveway. A quick call to Wila confirmed it was fine, just fine, to bring Derek to Penny's place after Francine relayed Dani's worry her dead husband might show up on her doorstep.

After she hung up, Francine released a deep breath. Hands-free phones. Best thing ever invented for a busy Soccer Mom of the Apocalypse.

Francine turned into her own driveway. Brittany raced out with her backpack slung over her right shoulder. She paused long enough to touch the biometric scanner to lock the house's front door before she ran to the minivan's passenger door. She yanked it open and clambered up into the front seat.

"Mom, Justine's really freaking out," Brittany said breathlessly as she pulled the door shut.

"I know she is, sweetie." Francine glanced at her daughter before she backed out of their drive. "And I'm sorry for not doing our day out like we planned."

"It's okay." Brittany shoved the latch plate of her seatbelt into the buckle with a snap. "Is it true her dead grandma showed up at their house this morning?"

Francine shifted the transmission into drive and accelerated down their street. "Yes." Admitting the truth wasn't easy, but Francine, Wila, and Dani were going to have to come clean with their children before they were forced to like Penny had been. Francine assumed she'd have a good time this weekend to talk to her daughter about the whole Soccer Moms of the Apocalypse thing.

The dead already rising from their graves ruined that plan.

"It sounds like the Hudsons need our moral support more than we needed our nails done," Brittany murmured.

Francine never had been more proud of her daughter than she was at this moment. "Yes, they do. That's what the emergency call from Penny was about this morning."

"I'm really glad all four of my grandparents are alive," Brittany added. "I couldn't imagine what I would do in Justine's situation . . ."

"What's wrong, sweetie?" Francine glanced at Brittany again. Her daughter had turned pale. So pale, her hair had an antique gold sheen against her skin.

Francine drove past the gates to their community and waved at Jim in the guardhouse before she flipped the right turn signal and braked for the stop sign at the exit. "Honey, what is it?"

"That's the real reason you're picking up the guys, isn't it?" A choked sound erupted from Brittany. "You and the rest of the moms are afraid Mark's dad will show up at his house."

"It's a definite concern," Francine answered grimly. "You saw how bothered Justine was. Her mom and grandpa are a lot worse, and I can only imagine how her dad will react when he finds out about his mom."

"Do you think Gene will end up in the funny farm?"

The question made Francine press the accelerator harder than she intended as she turned onto the street. She could have sworn she heard Sable whinny in protest. Once the minivan's speed was legal again, Francine glanced at her daughter.

"Brittany, that's not a very nice thing to say," Francine chided. "Mental health problems are just as serious as physical health problems." The odds were one of their children might end up in psychiatric care with the insanity of the Four Horsemen, ur, Four Horsewomen—

Oh, screw it! Wila was right. The Soccer Moms of the Apocalypse had a much nicer ring. Maybe she was on to something as far as public relations went.

"Justine's worried she'll end up in the hospital like her dad," Brittany said softly.

"I really doubt that will happen," Francine reassured her daughter despite her own misgivings.

"Is it true some weirdo kidnapped her?" Brittany's voice trembled.

Francine wished she could lie. There was enough ugly stuff in life without throwing demons into the mix. But a comforting falsehood now could put Brittany's life in even more danger.

"Yes, but we got her back safe and sound, and the man who kidnapped her won't be able to touch her again," Francine finished fiercely.

"So when you guys call yourselves the Soccer Moms of the Apocalypse, it's not some stupid name you made up, is it?"

Francine resisted the urge to groan. She should have known her brilliant daughter would put everything together. But the incessant questions now were worse than the constant "why"s when her daughter was three.

"No, it's not." Francine sighed. "But the whole situation is scary enough for us. Wila thought we needed a different moniker than the Four Horsemen of the Apocalypse."

"Horsemen? Like from the Bible?" Brittany almost sounded . . . happy?

"You're not scared?" Francine braked a little too hard for the red light ahead. Sable revved her engine in protest. "Sorry, girl." Francine patted the dashboard.

"Ohmigod! Is our minivan secretly your horse?" Brittany would have been jumping in her seat if it weren't for the belt securing her in place. "Is she black too? Can I ride her?"

Francine stared at her daughter. "That's what you're taking from all this? You want to ride my horse?"

"Well, you and dad said I couldn't get a real horse because we didn't have any place to keep her, but if your horse lives in our garage, then it's not a problem, right?" Brittany held her hands up in an innocent gesture.

"Sweetie, this is serious—"

The person behind them laid on their horn, and Francine jumped. People gave minivan moms such crap about their driving, but guys in their raised pickups were just as bad. The driver laid on his horn again.

Francine checked to make sure the traffic light was green before she tapped the accelerator. The pickup truck behind her continued tailgating her as they rolled down Baxter Street.

"Mom, I know your situation is serious, but as a Soccer Mom, don't you have superpowers and the horse?" Brittany continued, oblivious to the crazy guy in the truck behind them.

Francine flipped the left turn signal for Dani's subdivision and eased into the appropriate lane. The pickup performed the same maneuver as if their vehicles were connected.

"What do you mean by superpowers?" Francine said as she watched her mirrors. What if it was another demon driving the truck? She could only see a coat sleeve sticking out of the driver side window reflected in her mirrors. If it was a demon and she stopped at Dani's house now, the demons would know where she lived, too.

"That would depend on which Soccer Mom you are." Brittany was staring intently at her phone. "Oh, wow! Black is the color of Famine's horse." She looked up at Francine. "Do you make people starve to death? How does that work?"

Francine snorted. "Usually I just whack demons over the head with my scales."

The instant the traffic light switched from red to the green left turn arrow, Mr. Pickup blared his horn again.

"What is that guy's problem?" Brittany peered over her shoulder.

"That's an excellent question." Francine twisted the steering wheel and pressed the accelerator. Mr. Pickup stayed on their tail as they made the turn. He could just be an asshole, not a demon. That comparison though didn't make her feel any better. Humans could be even more evil than demons.

Otherwise, Uncle Oscar wouldn't have climbed into her bed when she was in kindergarten and done things to her.

She shoved the pain and embarrassment away. Mom and Dad had believed her when no one else had. That meant everything. And they kept him away from her. She didn't find out until years later they made sure he ended up in prison for what he did.

The guy behind her was just another bully like all the others in her life.

She wove through the various streets, deliberately avoiding Dani's house. The developer building this subdivision had gone into bankruptcy. There were empty lots at the back of the property.

The smart move would be to head back to Baxter Street and call 9-1-1. But part of her was really tired of playing the quiet girl and the perfect wife. The other part simply wanted to bash in this guy's head for acting like a dick. But she needed to be concerned about Brittany's safety, not her own impulses.

"Sable, I'm going to check out the guy behind us." Francine patted the dashboard again. "If he's a demon, I need you to take Brittany straight back to Penny's house."

"We can't leave you behind, Mom!" Brittany protested.

The minivan engine made a strange rattle that sounded like an additional objection.

"I am not putting you at risk," Francine snapped. "I could barely handle Justine's kidnapping. I would totally lose it if something happened you."

"Mom, are you okay?" Brittany whispered.

A quick glance at her fingers wrapped around the steering wheel showed shrunken, brittle skin over her bones. Well, crap. "This is what I look like when my Famine superpowers activate."

Brittany continued to stare at her. "I think we need to go trick-or-treating this year. You would scare the hell out of Kenny Lasser."

"First, we need to take care of our current problems," Francine muttered. "Remember what I said, Sable. And Brittany, stay with her if she's a horse or stay in that seat if she's a minivan."

"Yes, ma'am," Brittany murmured.

Francine pressed the accelerator and jerked the steering wheel to the right to parallel park in front of one of the empty lots. Her door was already open before she slammed on the brakes and shoved the gear into park. She flipped up the hood of her robe because she was too damn angry to shove Famine back into her hole, jumped out of her seat, and charged toward the truck.

The other driver climbed down from his cab. His jeans barely stayed on him because his belly seemed determined to overwhelm his belt. His steel-toed boots, brown hunting coat and black and red plaid flannel shirt completed his ensemble.

Just one problem—he wasn't a demon.

"What the hell is your issue?" she shouted as she approached him.

"Bitches like you shouldn't be on the road," he yelled back.

"So, you're being rude for the sake of rude?" She stopped and glared up at him.

His expression shifted from anger to apprehension. "What the hell is wrong with you? You look like you've got mange."

"You want to know what's wrong with me, big boy?" Francine seized the man's wrist. Panic flooded her, but it wasn't her emotions.

Instead of the ugliness of a demon that she half-expected, she saw the chipped ruby of his soul. The crystal strands that connected his soul to his body were equally damaged.

His recent memories flashed through her. His name was Jason, and he'd lost his construction job in favor of the boss's nephew. He didn't tell his wife. They were on the verge of losing their house, and he didn't know what to do. He couldn't tell Monica. His kids were about to be homeless, and there was a gun under the truck's bench seat. He planned to drive out to his favorite fishing spot, and try to make his death look like an accident so Monica and the kids would get the insurance money. Or maybe it would be easier to go to the construction site, shoot the boss and his nephew, and force the police to kill him. His story explained the chipping and cracking of his brilliant red soul.

Francine's anger melted away. She let go of the other driver. He stared at her while tears ran down his cheeks and into his dark bushy beard.

"That isn't the way to fix your problems, Jason," Francine murmured.

"What-what did you do to me? How did you change clothes?"

Francine pushed back her hood. The hood of her insulated teal L.L. Bean coat, not Famine's robes. She tucked her hair behind her ears. "I saw your troubles. I want to help."

"I don't need charity." He half-sobbed and half-snarled.

"It's not charity." She shoved her left hand in her coat pocket. "You do the work on your pickup?"

Jason shrugged. "My brother helped."

"There's an opening in the mechanics' department at the South Side Astin dealership." She pulled a business card from her pocket and held it out to him. "Talk to Roy Gage, the manager of the department. Tell him the boss's wife sent you."

Jason blinked as he accepted the business card, his mind obviously having trouble reconciling everything that was happening. "I don't have my certification—"

"If you're capable and show up on time, the dealership will subsidize your classes and testing."

"B-but—"

Francine held up a hand. "You don't have to stay forever. Think of your little ones at home. Take the opportunity to catch up on your bills while you look for something else." She shrugged. "But you might find you like working for my husband's company."

"Okay." He stared at the business card.

"But there is one condition, Jason."

"What?" His eyes narrowed.

"Stop honking at other drivers and tailgating them because you're having a bad day." She smiled. "A little kindness goes a long way in today's world."

He remained silent.

She pivoted and walked back to her minivan. Well, she'd done the best she could. She hoped she had gotten through to him. Maybe she should have taken his gun away in case he changed his mind about hurting himself or someone else.

"Miz Astin?" Jason called out.

Francine turned to look at him. For the first time in years, she didn't correct someone about her surname. "Yes?"

He held up the card. "Thanks."

She nodded before she continued walking. When she climbed into the minivan's driver seat, Brittany stared at her.

"What did you say to him, Mom?"

"I tried the Golden Rule." Francine tapped the hands-free phone control. "Please be quiet while I make a quick call."

A few seconds later, Roy answered his phone with a cheerful, "What can I do for you today, Mrs. Coy-Astin?"

"I think I may have found a new mechanic for you." She rattled off Jason's information.

"This is great if he works out," Roy said. "My other three guys are about to mutiny, even with the overtime pay."

"He will," Francine assured him.

She just prayed Jason wouldn't do anything else stupid the rest of the day.

Chapter 6

Once Francine and Brittany picked up the boys and lunch for everyone, they headed back to Penny's house. Unfortunately, Gene's car was already in the Hudsons' driveway. But so was Father Perez's tiny electric hatchback. Once again, Francine parallel parked at the curb in front of the Hudsons' home.

Francine and the kids grabbed bags of takeout and marched up to the porch and through the front door. The silent tension in the house was palpable.

In the kitchen, Gene sat with his arms crossed and scowled at Laura, who wore a pair of Penny's sweats and a cardigan over a t-shirt. Edward sat beside his son, the farthest he could get from his resurrected wife without leaving the room. Poor Penny looked miserable, and Justine had obviously been crying. That explained the tension.

Father Perez stood. "Taco Man is my favorite! What can I do to help?" His forced cheer was wasted on the Hudsons.

So were his smoldering good looks and sweet disposition. If he wasn't a priest, he'd be a perfect boyfriend for Dani.

"Why don't you help Penny with plates and utensils?" Francine said. "Kids, go wash up."

"Ah, ma-a-an," Derek whined. "Are we getting regulated to the basement again?"

"Nope, you are sitting in on this meeting, but I want clean hands if you're touching my tacos," Francine ordered.

"This doesn't involve our children," Gene bit out.

Francine set her bags on the counter and whirled to face him. "Yes, it does. You put Justine in danger because you let your ego get in the way. I'm not letting you do the same with Brittany or the boys."

"Does Neal even know what you are?" Gene snapped.

"Yes, he does," Francine replied calmly as she took off her coat and slung it over the back of a kitchen chair. "And I have to say, he took it a lot better than you." She waved in Penny's direction. "I could understand if your wife looked as scary as me or Dani. But she doesn't, so I don't get why your tighty-whities are in a wad."

"Neal's seen you when you . . .changed." Surprise covered Gene's face.

"I showed him because I didn't need him accusing me of lying to him," Francine said. "Speaking of which—" She turned to face Penny. "Have you checked Laura's soul?"

"My what?" Laura spluttered.

"Her what?" Penny said.

"Seriously?" Father Perez looked at Francine in amazement.

"Father Perez, can I borrow you for a sec so Penny can see what a normal soul looks like?" Francine asked.

"Will it hurt?" he asked tentatively.

"It's . . . uncomfortably intimate." Francine decided that was the best way to describe it. "The thing is you'll see and feel my soul, too."

"When did you start seeing souls?" Penny carried plates over to the table.

"This morning—" Francine started.

"Yeah, this asshole in a raised pickup was tailgating us for no reason," Brittany blurted as she and Justine re-entered the kitchen from the hallway.

"Language, young lady." Francine raised an eyebrow.

"Well, he was until you touched him, and then he started crying—" Brittany explained.

"Men don't cry," Mark said as he and Derek re-entered the kitchen from the utility room. Dani's son tossed his black, glossy bangs out of his equally dark eyes.

"This guy was," Brittany said crossly.

"But my uncle says—" Mark started to argue.

"Son, every man cries at some point in their life," Edward said. "I cried the day my wife said yes to my marriage proposal, the days my sons and grandchildren were born, and the day I lost my wife." He eyed Francine. "What happened with this guy?"

"How about everyone fill their plates and have a seat at the table?" She looked at each person in turn. "Then we'll explain everything." She focused on Gene. "We promise."

"What do I need to do?" Father Perez asked.

"Let me hold your hand." Francine grinned. "Like in the Beatles' song."

"The Beatles?" The priest laughed. "We really need to update your taste in music." But he held out his hand to her.

"Take a deep breath—" Francine clasped his hand. This time, the transition was much easier. She gasped.

Father Perez's soul was a lovely yellow-white gleaming diamond with zillions of tinier diamonds connecting his soul to his body. The yellowish cast wasn't a flaw. Nor was this soul cracked like poor Jason's. His soul made her feel warm and joyful. She felt a hand on her shoulder.

"Ohmigod," Penny breathed. "That's incredible."

Francine released Father Perez's hand. Her sight returned to normal.

"Wow," he murmured. "I wish I could do that. It would be so much easier to counsel parishioners at the church."

"That is so much cooler than my bow," Penny added.

"Oh, awesome!" Brittany plopped down on the chair next Justine. "Your mom's Pestilence. Mine's Famine." Her eyes narrowed, and the corner of her mouth tilted as she worked things out. "That means Derek's mom is War, and Mark's mom is Death."

"What are you talking about?" Mark shot Brittany a quizzical look.

"Our moms are the Four Horsemen of the Apocalypse," Justine blurted. "Or as they prefer, the Four Soccer Moms of the Apocalypse."

"So that's really happened to our kitchen chair!" Derek's teeth flashed white against his dark skin. "Doesn't War have a flaming sword?"

Penny turned to Francine. "I know Dani's on her way, but I thought we were waiting until Wila got here after her shift."

Francine shrugged. "Justine already knows and Brittany and Derek figured it out on their own. We need to fess up now."

Mark sat down on the chair closest to Edward. "I thought the Four Horsemen were supposed to be the bad guys."

"You're Catholic, dude." Derek made a face at him as he plopped onto the chair on the other side of Mark. "Don't you read the Bible?"

"Actually, they—" Father Perez started.

"Okay, kids." Francine gestured sharply to include the priest. "Let's stop before one of us says something we will all regret." She turned to Laura. "Will you allow us to take a look at your soul? Just to make sure?"

Laura swallowed hard before she nodded. "I guess I need to know, too."

"Mind if I take the lead on this one?" Penny asked.

"Of course," Francine said at the same time Laura said, "Please."

Penny held out her hand, and Laura clasped her daughter-in-law's fingers. Francine laid her hand on Penny's shoulder.

Laura's soul was the deepest, greenest emerald Francine had ever seen. It was cut and polished, and it gleamed with an inner brilliance. Any concerns she had about the dead being part of the demons' plans to destroy the world disappeared.

But the difference between her soul and the men's were the connectors to the body weren't matching crystals. In Laura's case, the connectors were strands of matching green light.

Francine's vision switched back to normal, and she released Penny's shoulder. On the other hand, Penny grabbed her mother-in-law in a tight hug.

"It's you. It's really you." Penny straightened and wiped the wetness from her face.

Laura accepted a handkerchief Edward handed to her over Mark's head for her own tears.

Penny shot Francine an odd look, but Francine shook her head. They'd have to discuss the difference in the connectors between soul and body later. There was no point in alarming Laura and the rest of her family at this moment.

Francine nodded as her stomach rumbled. "Time for tacos and truth."

Chapter 7

Over delicious, crunchy beef and cheese tacos, Francine and Penny laid out everything that had happened over the last three weeks since Dani drove the atrocious puke green minivan off Neal Astin's Central Oakfield dealership lot.

"In other words, Mom panicked," Mark mumbled around a mouthful of taco.

"Dude, that's gross!" Justine glared at him. "Don't talk with food in your mouth."

Her statement only prodded Mark to open his mouth wide to show half-masticated taco.

Francine shot him her best disapproving mom expression.

He closed his mouth, finished chewing, and swallowed before he added, "Mom's afraid my dad may show up at our house, isn't she?"

"Yes, she is," Francine said. "And Derek's mom and her partner already ran into someone they weren't able to save last year. More people may be coming back."

Mark slowly blinked. "B-but the dead come back right before the world ends, right?"

"That's one of the interpretations," Francine said.

"But something you all need to remember is that the Horsemen, ur, Soccer Moms," Father Perez amended. "They work with Christ to save people from the bad guys, Mark."

"Are you saying Jesus is already here?" Gene asked.

"Wouldn't it be wild if Coach Cordero was the real Jesus?" Derek grinned.

"That's—" Gene abruptly shut up and stared at his uneaten tacos.

"Gene, no one's asking you to change your beliefs," Penny said.

"Except—" He waved his hand in a helpless gesture to indicate the three adult women at the table.

"Humans don't understand everything in the universe," Francine said. "If you want to look at it scientifically, demons are a type of parasite, and we happen to be the exterminators."

"Then what am I?" Laura asked.

Francine shrugged. "For all we know, humans enter a type of hibernation, and we've been killing ourselves by burying people."

"Dios mio!" Father Perez shouted. "You can't be seriously coddling him!"

The kids snickered at the priest swearing.

"Just because you say it in Spanish doesn't mean it's appropriate in front of children," Francine snapped.

"Don't sweat it, Miz Francine," Derek proclaimed. "We hear a lot worse at school."

"That wasn't the point Francine was trying to make." Laura scowled at the boy.

Ed cleared his throat. "No offense was intended, Padre. My son has had some peculiar ideas since he came home from college."

"Stop!" Penny glared at everyone in turn. "All of you. You are not turning my kitchen into the Thirty Years War!"

"Penny's right," Francine said. "We need to focus on the more immediate issue, which is the kids' safety."

"What do you mean?" Mark protested. "Derek and I were perfectly fine, playing video games. If a zombie showed up, we would have defended our house."

"Really?" Francine considered her words. Dani hadn't done Mark any favors by letting her brother and her dad be her son's primary male figures in his life. "Take a good look at Grandma Hudson. What if it wasn't your dad who showed up on your front porch? What if it was your Abuelita Hernandez?"

Mark stared at the last taco on his plate. The poor kid barely remembered his dad, but his paternal grandmother had died in her sleep last January. And the memory of Olivia hit a little harder since she had taken care of Mark after school until Dani got home from work.

"That's different." Mark sniffed. He swiped his sleeve across his face in an attempt to cover up the tear or two that had escaped.

"This is difficult for all of us," Francine said. "But you kids need to be extra careful. It's not the resurrected people you need to be afraid of. Demons have been possessing people in town."

"Do we need to come up with code words like in kindergarten so we know our parents sent someone to get us?" Derek asked.

Penny turned to Francine. "While that's a good idea, it's not going to work if our adult family members get possessed."

"It won't," Gene admitted.

"We need to carry symbols of our belief. That'll help prevent possession." Edward grimaced. "I don't know what to do about Gene."

"Thanks, Dad," Gene grumbled.

"We may have another problem," Father Perez said. "Demons can't possess the dead, but what happens if they are resurrected like Mrs. Hudson? You confirmed she has her soul."

"It's there, but—" Francine shot a glance at Penny.

Penny groaned as she leaned back in her chair and stared at the ceiling. "This is getting more and more complicated." She faced Father Perez again. "The connections holding Laura's soul to her body are different than a living person's."

"What do you mean?" Laura's alarm was a palpable thing in the room. "What's wrong with me?"

"Not wrong, different," Francine said. "We don't know what it means, but we'll figure this out. We have to."

The doorbell sang the tune to "Rudolph the Red-Nosed Reindeer." All the kids started laughing.

"Anyone home?" Dani's voice bounced past the staircase and down the hallway.

"We're in the kitchen!" Penny yelled.

Dani stalked into the kitchen, followed by Marian.

All the Hudsons, the kids, and Father Perez froze in place.

While Dani still sported her royal blue business suit, the attractive elderly woman with her wore black wool slacks that contrasted with her cream-colored cashmere coat. A designer purse was slung over her shoulder.

Marion smiled brightly and held up the plastic bags in her hands. "I didn't realize you had a full house this afternoon. It's a good thing I brought extra ice cream." She walked over to Edward and pecked him on the lips. "Hi, sweetie."

Laura's jaw dropped.

Francine couldn't stop watching the train wreck that was happening before her eyes.

Marian set the bags on a bare spot on the table before she turned to Laura and held out her hand. "I'm sorry. We haven't met. I'm Marian Clark, Edward's girlfriend."

Laura's eyes narrowed, and she found her voice. "Laura Hudson. Ed's wife."

Chapter 8

Francine looked up at Dani, who gave a helpless shrug.

"We pulled up in front of the house at the same time," Dani whispered.

Marian turned back to Edward with a shocked expression. "You told me your wife died."

"Until a few hours ago, she was dead," Edward snapped.

Penny stood up. "Before everyone gets upset, there's an explanation for all this."

"Why would you lie to me?" Marian's voice dropped an octave, and her face blazed a color that could only be described as nuclear red.

"I didn't lie!" Edward threw his hands in the air.

"Kids, grab spoons, grab the ice cream, and head downstairs," Francine barked.

"I knew we were going to get banned to the basement," Derek grumbled.

"We're not missing anything," Mark pseudo-whispered. "You should hear my mom and Uncle Marty when my Grandpa Chuck has one of his girlfriends come to Sunday dinner."

"Marcos Emmanuel Elante!" Dani's cheeks turned a dark rose, and she pointed at the basement door. "Downstairs! Now!"

"Yes, ma'am," he muttered.

Francine had to bite her tongue to keep from laughing when Mark made a point of grabbing the bags of ice cream as he left the table. Derek followed the food. Brittany had the presence of mind to take her plate to the sink and rinse it before she grabbed a wad of napkins. Justine retrieved spoons, and trailed after Brittany down the stairs.

And the kids made a point of leaving the basement door open so they could eavesdrop.

"Is anyone going to tell me what the hell is going on here?" Marian snapped.

"Take a seat, Miz Clark," Francine said as she pushed to her own feet and crossed the kitchen to close the basement door. "Would you like some coffee?"

"I'd prefer answers." Marian scowled at Laura, then Edward.

"You can't tell her the truth," Father Perez said. "We could inadvertently start a panic."

"What truth?" Marian made a point of sitting next to Edward, which earned her an ugly glare from Laura.

"If the Fifth Seal has broken like the padre and the Soccer Moms believe, my mother and Wila's patient can't be the only people rising from their graves," Gene said.

Penny stared at her husband, her expression somewhere between shock and pleasure that he was starting to take the situation seriously.

Francine returned and laid her hand on Penny's left shoulder. "Why don't you make everyone some coffee while Dani and I deal with the remnants of lunch?"

"Can't I get some tacos first?" Dani waved at the remaining Taco Man bags.

"Sure," Francine said. "Help me clear the table first, and then get yourself a clean plate."

Dani cocked her head. "When did you and Penny exchange personalities?"

"This morning at the crack of dawn when she called me in a panic about her dead mother-in-law standing on her front porch."

Over coffee and the remaining tacos, Francine explained everything to Edward's girlfriend. When she finished the tale of the Soccer Moms, the demons, and the rising dead, Marian blushed.

"I'm sorry, Laura." She swallowed audibly. "I want you to know I don't sleep with married men."

"I can't fault you for assuming I was out of the way." Laura favored Marian with a gracious smile. "But I'm here now."

Edward jerked to his feet. "But for how long, Laura? Do you have any idea of what the boys and I went through by losing you? I can't do this! Not again!" He stomped out of the kitchen. A few seconds later, a door slamming reverberated through the entire house.

His tirade seemed to take the steam out of both women's sails.

"I can understand his feelings." Marian looked at Francine. "Does this mean my husband Dennis might show up on my doorstep?"

"It might, depending on where he is buried," Francine said.

Marian gave a nervous little laugh. "He wanted to be cremated. I scattered his ashes on Maui. That's where we had our honeymoon."

"So far, we haven't had anyone show up who was cremated," Francine said. "And he would have to cross half of the Pacific Ocean and a good chunk of the continental U.S. to end up at your house."

Laura cleared her throat. "Are you living in the same house? Because when I first woke up this morning, I went to our old place, and the lady who lives there now was ready to call the police."

"I sold our house and bought a condo," Marian murmured.

"You'd go back to him?" Gene asked.

"Eugene Crawford Hudson, you mind your tongue!" Laura snapped. "This situation is difficult enough for everyone, and I raised you to be better than this."

"Father Perez, would you mind taking Gene and your coffee to the living room?" Francine said. "The Soccer Moms need to have some girl time with Laura and Marian."

"I will not be put out of my own kitchen," Gene growled.

The priest stood with his large cup of hazelnut coffee tight in his grip. "*Ese*, do really want to cross your mother *and* three of the Four Horsemen?"

Francine coughed not-so-discreetly.

He glanced at her with a self-deprecating grin. "Sorry, three of the Four Soccer Moms."

Gene's jaw clenched, but he rose to his feet, grabbed his mug of coffee with vanilla and caramel creamer, and marched down the hallway toward his office. Penny rolled her eyes at her husband's spite. However, Father Perez followed him.

Francine returned her attention to the two older women. "Laura, it might be best if you come stay at my house tonight."

"I understand some things have changed, but—" Laura looked helplessly at Penny. "You would choose her over me?" She waved in Marian's direction.

"This isn't a question of my choice or Edward's," Penny said. "None of us know how to handle this. After I lost my parents while I was in college, you were as much a mother to me as you were to Gene and Theo. I-I—" She choked on her words and gulped her pumpkin spice latte. "I held your hand when you passed, I picked out that suit for you to wear, and-and I'm falling apart right now."

"Laura, we are trying to figure out how to stop the end of the world," Francine said. "Not to be nasty or dismissive, but the Soccer Moms need Penny more than you do at the moment, and we need Pestilence with her head on straight. Also, I need an experienced demon hunter to help me with my research because Edward's definitely lost his focus considering the tantrum he just threw, and Father Perez has his hands full keeping Gene from doing anything stupid. That means I need you with me."

Laura frowned. "You said the four of you took out a demon nest earlier this week."

"That was just one nest," Francine said. "We're sure more will be coming.

I need your expertise. Between you and Father McAvoy, maybe we'll have a shot at winning our battle."

"All right." Laura nodded. "But could we stop and get me some clean underwear on the way to your house? My others were . . . I threw them out."

Francine grinned. "Not a problem. Brittany and I had planned a shopping expedition this afternoon anyway."

Chapter 9

Francine was glad Brittany decided to spend the night with Justine. All of the Hudsons needed some emotional support after the day they'd had. Most especially the woman sitting in the passenger seat of Francine's minivan/horse.

"Do you think Ed loves this Marian more than he loved me?" Laura asked.

"Do you love Gene more than you love Theo?" Francine replied.

Laura chuckled. "All right. Point taken." She sighed. "I never thought I was the jealous type. But seeing her walk up to my husband and lay one straight on the lips in front of my son and his family made me want to-to—"

"Slap her upside the head?" Francine offered.

"Actually, I was thinking more of a roundhouse kick to the head followed by a leg sweep and yanking her arm out of the socket."

"Uh, I, uh . . ." Francine glanced at her passenger. Laura Hudson had always struck her as a prim and proper, old-fashioned, stay-at-home mother. "I didn't know you practiced martial arts."

Laura snorted. "Knew a few of the disciplines before I ever met Ed. After we were married, he didn't want the boys to know about our demon hunting. But I still took classes when the boys were at school or on my supposed bridge nights."

Francine grinned. "That certainly explains a lot."

"What do you mean?"

"You were super supportive of Penny when she opened Java's Palace."

"I made a decision to give up my dreams," Laura said. "Ed wanted a normal life for our children, and I don't regret my choices. But Penny was the closest thing I ever had to a daughter, and I didn't want her to make the same mistakes I did."

"That sounds like regret to me,"

"Maybe it is." Laura sighed.

"What about Theo's wife Alexis?" Francine asked.

"We are, well, were, cordial." Laura laughed again. "It wasn't until Alexis and Theo started dating I realized why Ed found my hippy background so annoying. But I didn't rub my friends' and family's noses in my ideals. I almost broke down and served her veal just to piss her off."

Francine joined in with Laura's laughter. "That would have been worth seeing the look on her face." Alexis believed if her friends and family didn't support her cause du jour, it was a personal betrayal. Francine had her own urge to throttle Alexis at last year's Fourth of July party when she whined about the real hamburgers touching her dang soy burger, which Neal made an extra effort to buy and grill for her.

They turned onto Baxter Street and headed for Waterford Crossing.

Laura cleared her throat. "Speaking of Theo, has anyone told him about me yet?"

"No," Francine said. "At least, I don't think so. Your mother rising from the grave isn't something that should be handled over the phone."

"No, I suppose not."

A quick glance showed Laura staring pensively out the passenger window.

"I'm sorry this isn't the homecoming you deserve," Francine said.

"I don't know what I expected." A self-deprecating chuckle burbled out of the older woman. "I would have been just as freaked out if any of my dead relatives showed up at my front door."

"Actually, you probably would have karate-chopped the hell out of them."

Instead of laughing at Francine's lame attempt to joke, Laura turned back to staring out the passenger window. "Maybe. Or maybe I would have fallen to my knees and begged their forgiveness for not saving them."

Francine kept her mouth shut the rest of the way to the shopping center. Whatever button she accidentally pushed had disturbed her guest, and that simply wasn't good manners.

Francine browsed through the women's section of the department store while Laura tried on her selections. Francine's phone rang. Relief swept through her when the caller ID flashed "Neal". As much as she loved her friends, she didn't think she could handle another crisis today.

"Hi, honey! What's up?"

"You probably already know this, but people are coming out of their graves in all the county's cemeteries."

Francine replaced the blouse she'd been considering to its rack. "More than the Oakfield Cemetery?"

"Yeah, there was a special report on the news. Both the sheriff's department and the Oakfield PD are advising everyone to go home and lock their doors."

"Are you sending the staff home?"

"Yeah, I'm cutting them loose at three this afternoon so everyone can get home before sundown."

Francine glanced at the entrance to the dressing rooms. "Are there any reports of the dead doing anything wrong?"

"Not so far," Neal admitted. "They seem confused. Many of them are going back to where they used to live from what the news report said. I'm glad our parents are alive and well in Florida. Can you imagine having a dead relative showing up on your doorstep?"

"Uh, there's something I was going to call you about when I was finished at Waterston's."

Neal laughed. "Let me guess. Brittany wants to buy the entire junior miss section."

"No." Francine pinched the bridge of her nose. "Gene's mom needs to stay with us a couple of days."

"Gene's mom? Did I hear you correctly? Gene Hudson's mother, right? The dead one."

"Yes." Francine could imagine Neal's face right now. "Laura showed up at Gene and Penny's house this morning after she couldn't find Edward at their old place."

"Shit," Neal muttered.

"That about sums it up." Francine glanced at the entrance to the dressing rooms. Still no Laura. "It didn't help when the lady Edward has been seeing dropped by, so I said Laura could stay with us."

"How are you doing?" Neal said.

"Surprisingly, I'm the one trying to keep the other Soccer Moms from flipping out." Francine looked around, but no one was close enough to hear her conversation. "Wila ran into a DOA case she responded to last year, and Dani's paranoid Heath will show up at her place."

"For Mark's sake, I can understand Dani's feelings."

"Does this mean you're not going to give me crap for bringing a dead woman home?"

"Sweetheart, I never had a doubt you could take care of yourself before you became Famine. If you think this is the right thing to do, I'm behind you all the way." Neal's words tickled Francine to her toes.

"Thank you for believing in me," she said.

"I do have another question though," Neal added. "Is the Jason Matthews who showed up for an interview with Roy at Southside a dead guy, too?"

"He showed up?" A surge of relief flooded through Francine. "That's fantastic!"

"What's not fantastic is the story he told me," Neal said. "Was he really road raging at you with Brittany in the minivan?"

"Honey, he'd lost his job and was planning to commit suicide when we encountered each other," she said softly. "Please give him a chance. He's got two little kids to raise and no other prospects."

"How do you know this? Did he tell you?"

"I had a new power show up. I could see his soul. Deep down, he's a good person. He just had a few bad breaks over the last couple of months."

"You know if anybody else told me this kind of stuff, I'd be calling Gene for a referral." Neal chuckled.

"That's not funny," Francine chided. "Between Penny and his mom, I'm worried Gene's going to end up in the psych ward himself. He's not handling any of this well."

"Should I take him out for a beer tonight while you have a girls' night with Mrs. Hudson?" Neal asked.

"You can try, but don't be surprised if he refuses." Francine sighed. "Oh, and that was the other thing I was going to tell you. Brittany is spending the night at the Hudsons. Between the kidnapping and her grandmother, Justine needed a little moral support."

"Is Penny bringing the girls to tomorrow's game, or do we need to pick up Brittany early?"

"If you're going to the Hudsons tonight, you can take our daughter's gear to her."

"What a convenient excuse to take Gene out. Clever girl." Neal laughed. "Keep using your powers for good, babe."

"I promise." Francine frowned when Laura came out of the dressing room area with an armload of clothes. The older woman was putting more than half of them back. "I need to go, honey. Laura needs something to wear besides moldy grave clothes."

"Talk to you when I get home," Neal said. "Wait, should I pick up dinner on the way home?"

"No, I've got a chicken broccoli casserole in the freezer."

"Broccoli? No." He laughed again. "I love that you try to keep the entire family healthy, but today's events require something more. I'll put in an order at The Steak House. Love you!"

"Love you, too." Francine ended the call and stuck her phone in its slot on her tote before she marched over to Laura. "What's wrong with all these?"

"I can't let you buy clothes for me." Laura looked like she was on the verge of tears. "I can't pay you back."

"Hey." Francine put up a hand to stop Laura from hanging up the jeans she selected. "First of all, I'm happy to help because I know Penny would do the same with my mom and mother-in-law if they were in your position. Secondly, you have a lovely hourglass shape. My pants are not going to fit you. Otherwise, I'd let you raid my closet. Last of all, public nudity is still illegal in Illinois."

"B-but—" Laura's features pinched at her embarrassment.

"We have no idea what happens next," Francine murmured. "Or how long you will be here. A couple of outfits is a small price to pay."

Finally, Laura nodded. "All right. I'll look for a job on Monday to pay you back."

It was best to ignore her statement. If the dead continued to rise, the county would probably call a state of emergency. No sense worrying Laura about finding employment by pointing out the obvious.

"Let's swing by Java's Palace." Francine grinned. "I don't know about you, but I need coffee and biscotti after a busy afternoon of shopping."

Chapter 10

When Francine and Laura entered Java's Palace, Josie manned the cash register.

"I hear you got a promotion," Francine said. "Congratulations!"

The college student blushed a deep rose, a far darker hue than her cotton candy-colored hair. "Thanks, Ms. Coy-Astin. You want your usual?"

"Let's change things up." Francine examined the board behind the new assistant manager. "I'd like a large snickerdoodle latte and two cinnamon biscotti sticks." She turned to Laura. "What sounds good to you?"

"A large chai tea and a cranberry-orange muffin, please."

Josie grinned as she handed Francine her receipt. "Why don't you ladies sit down in the dining room, and we'll bring your orders out to you?"

"Thanks." Francine tossed her receipt in her tote. It was a good thing Penny took the rest of the week off to be with Justine after the kidnapping. Otherwise, Penny would be driving her staff bonkers. Also, it was good for Josie's confidence to man the store herself. The girl was blossoming under Penny's mentorship.

Francine and Laura strolled over to a free booth along one of the huge picture windows. Curiosity at the older woman's bemused smile made Francine ask, "What is so funny?"

Laura shrugged. "I think I was born a couple of generations too early. Even my dad with his ratty ponytail would have flipped out over Josie's pink hair, but I wish I could have done such a color."

"So why didn't you after you moved out of your parents' house?" Francine smiled. "You were working and had your own money."

Laura sighed. "I made a lot of compromises when it came to Ed. Probably more than I should have."

"It sounds like you did all the compromising."

"He took good care of me and the boys. We wanted for nothing." The face Laura made indicated she was trying to convince herself.

"Except?" Francine didn't really want to pry, but Laura obviously needed someone to talk to about her bizarre situation.

"I never really got to explore the world like I wanted," she admitted. "There's a part of me that wants to say if I've been dead for the last couple of years, then our marriage is over, and I'm free. But the other side wants to smack the crap out of this Marian woman." Her expression turned pensive. "How long has Ed been seeing her?"

"A month or two, I think," Francine said. "You have to understand it really did take him a long time to get over you. She's the first woman he's shown any interest in since you passed."

"Does he love her?"

"I don't know." Francine shrugged. "That's something you and Edward need to discuss. Mind if I ask you something I've been curious about for years?"

"If I remember the answer." Laura smiled.

"How come you're the only one who calls him Ed?"

Laura laughed. "He was always worried about how clients perceived him, and he wanted to become a partner in the accounting firm where he was first employed. Outside of the work he did for the Vatican, that is. So he insisted on people calling him Edward."

Francine grinned. "I'm surprised he didn't get huffy with you about calling him by his full name."

"Oh, he tried to." Laura leaned forward. "I started calling him Bunny Rabbit in front of non-family. He dropped the issue. To me, he'll always be the farm kid from the Midwest who was good at numbers, demon hunting, and sex, but not much else."

Josie chose that moment to approach their table with their order on her tray. She obviously had heard the last little bit of Laura's statement from the way the assistant manager's cheeks flamed pink again.

The older woman grinned at the assistant manager. "Yes, sweetie. Old people have sex, too. That's how your mommy and daddy were born."

Josie set the snacks and hot drinks in front of Francine and Laura. "It's not that, ma'am. My roommate will tell you I'm not an appreciative audience when she tries to tell me about her sex life. Intimacy is between the people involved and no one else." She tucked the tray under her arm. "Anything else I can get for you ladies?"

"No, thank you." Francine smiled.

Josie nodded and stalked back toward the counter.

"Is it me, or did the feminist agenda slide backwards over the last fifty years?" Laura peeled the paper from her muffin.

"In some ways, it slid backwards." Francine dipped her biscotti in her extra large cup. "In others, it's gotten better. The worst part is half the female population thinks they can dictate what the other half should be doing."

Laura chuckled while she pulled apart her muffin. "Trading one dictator for another. I have to admit I was always surprised you and Penny became friends."

"So am I." Francine let the espresso and milk drip from the tip of the cinnamon biscotti. "But our relationship was more one of necessity."

"Necessity?"

"We were the only ones with daughters of the same age at the kids' preschool." Francine shrugged. "Brittany and Justine refused to play with dolls because they wanted to play trucks with the boys. The director had a fit, and the other moms let us know we were weird, but Wila backed us." She took a bite of her biscotti.

"Did you pull the girls from that preschool?" Laura popped a bite of muffin in her mouth.

"No, Gene and Penny called the owner and threatened to sue them for discrimination, and Neal and I said we would fund the lawsuit."

Laura shook her head, swallowed her bite, and washed it down with a sip of her tea. "Gene and Penny never told us about any problems with the daycare."

"Maybe because they were worried after Edward flipped out over Theo putting on your makeup and wearing your clothes."

"You know about that?" Laura winced.

"I know more about Edward's crap than I care to." Francine cocked her head. "Finding out about yours and his pasts with the Vatican did surprise me. You both put on a good front being a conservative suburban couple."

Laura sighed. "That may be exactly why our boys rebelled in the ways they did."

"It sounds like you did your own share of rebelling."

"I suppose I did." Laura leaned over and stared at something behind Francine.

She turned to look. An older Black woman was entering Java's Palace. A woman who looked as disheveled and dirty as Laura had when Francine arrived at the Hudsons' house this morning. At least, this lady had both of her orthopedic shoes tied firmly to her feet.

"Excuse me." The woman approached Josie at the counter. "Can I use your phone? My purse is missing, and my granddaughter wasn't home when I walked to her apartment."

Francine jumped up and approached the counter. "Josie, get this lady whatever she wants to eat and drink." She pulled her phone out of her pocket. "You can use my phone. And once you have something in your stomach, I can drive you wherever in town you need to go."

"Thank you—" The woman accepted the device, but she turned it this way and that as she looked at it. Her hand trembled. "You have one of those new smart phones. I've never used one of these before."

"Do you want me to call your granddaughter?"

"Yes, please. Her name's Wila." The woman swallowed hard. "Wila Jackson."

At the name, Francine froze and stared at the distraught woman. "Wila . . . Jackson?"

Crap. Jackson was Wila's ex-louse's name. And there weren't any other women with the same first name in Oakfield as far as Francine knew.

The disheveled woman nodded. Francine tapped the controls to pull up the contact information for Wila. She held up her phone for the woman to see the picture. "Is this your Wila?"

The woman broke into a broad smile. "That's my baby girl." She frowned. "Why the devil is she listed as Wila Ardale again?" She looked at Francine. "Did something happen to her husband Deion?"

"You could say that. I'm a friend of hers. Wila calls you Gammy, right?" At the woman's nod, Francine tapped the phone call icon.

After the third ring, Wila groaned. "I've had a very weird shift, and you just woke me up. This had better be good, Francine."

"I wanted to give a head's up before I drive to your place. I'm bringing your Gammy over."

Chapter 11

"You're what?"

Francine waved Wila's grandmother toward the counter. "Why don't you place your order? Then you might want to go to the restroom and wash up a little." She wished she knew the woman's name, but she had died ten years ago, and Wila only referred to her as Gammy.

And Gammy appeared very confused and upset. "Can't I talk to my granddaughter?"

"What the hell are you talking about, Francine?" Wila yelled over the receiver.

"Hold on." Francine tapped mute.

Thankfully, Laura stepped up to Francine's side and held out her hand. "Hi, I'm Laura Hudson. What's your name?"

"Latricia. Latricia Wilkinson." Gammy started to reach for Laura's hand and jerked back. "How on earth did I get this dirty?" She stared at the dirt caked under what was left of her fingernails.

"How do you take you coffee?" Josie smiled brightly.

"Black." Latricia stared at Francine. "Doesn't Wila want to talk to me?"

"I woke her up, and you know how coherent Wila is when she doesn't get enough sleep." Francine smiled. "Josie, can you fix Mrs. Wilkinson a breakfast sandwich, too, while I deal with Wila?"

"Sure thing!" The assistant manager smiled brightly.

Francine sighed in relief as Laura led Wila's grandmother back toward the public restroom. She unmuted her phone and raised it to her ear as she strode back to their booth.

"—swear to God I'm gonna shish kebab you if you don't answer me right this minute," Wila shrieked.

"Calm down," Francine murmured. "We're at the Palace, and it's a good thing, too. Your grandmother walked to your old apartment. When she couldn't find you, she came here to ask to use the phone."

"Oh, geez." Wila groaned. "I haven't lived at the Oak River Apartments in nine years, but the coffee shop would be on a direct line from Riverside Cemetery to the complex. Is she okay?"

"A little confused and shaken like Penny's mother-in-law was this morning." Francine glanced up as Josie delivered Mrs. Wilkinson's sandwich and black coffee. "Just a second." She reached into her purse for the cash for Gammy's order.

Josie held up her hand. "Penny called a minute ago and said you're covered since you're taking care of her mother-in-law and Wila's grandmother today."

Francine winced. "You told her, huh?"

Josie hugged herself. "She's not the first zombie to come in here today. Valerie's sister showed up. Poor thing walked all the way from the Oakfield Cemetery. I'm glad I came here for school." She shook her head. "I don't have to worry about my grandparents showing up at my apartment."

"Take the money and stick it in the tip jar," Francine insisted as she held up a couple of large denomination bills. "You and the rest of the staff have earned it if you've been dealing with the risen dead all day."

Josie accepted the money Francine held out to her. "Do you think some of the people on the news are right? That people rising from their graves is signaling the end of the world? Especially after what—" The girl swallowed hard. "I'm having nightmares about what the demons made us do."

Empathy fizzed along Francine's nerves. It was a wonder Penny's entire staff didn't quit after they were possessed and used to try to kill the Soccer Moms.

Francine smiled. "You know me, Penny, and our friends will do everything we can to prevent the world from ending." She fished in her tote and pulled out one of Father Perez's cards. "If you need to talk to someone who knows about the weird stuff, go to Saint Michael's. When you call, tell whoever answers the phone that I sent you."

Josie looked at the card for a long time before she nodded. "Thank you."

Francine raised her phone back to her ear. "Did you catch that?"

"The part where that pink-haired barista called my grandmother a zombie? Yeah!" Wila yelled.

"Would you please stop screaming in my ear?"

"I'm sorry." Wila sighed. "I'm not going to get anymore sleep with this stuff going on. For the first time in my life, I wish the ex-louse had Derek for the weekend."

"This isn't easy for anyone, but so far no one seems to be panicking, and none of the dead are eating brains."

"Ha. Ha. Ha."

Francine tapped her fingers on the tabletop. "I'll swing by the super store on the way to your place and pick up sweats, shoes, and undies for your grandmother to wear after she showers. I can take her shopping for more clothes tomorrow—"

"I can buy clothes for my own grandmother, thank you very much," Wila snapped.

"All right." Francine tried to keep her own irritation out of her voice. "If you can handle that, Laura and I are going to check out the town cemeteries to see if we can figure out things."

Wila cursed. "I'm sorry. Honestly, I wasn't trying to dump all the crazy stuff on you."

Holy cow! Wila Ardale apologizing? Yep, it was definitely the end of the world.

"I know you weren't." Francine spotted Laura and Mrs. Wilkinson returning from the bathroom. "We'll be there in an hour."

She tapped her phone to end the call, shoved it into her tote, and plastered a smile on her face. "Your sandwich and coffee are here."

"Thank you so much, dear." Mrs. Wilkinson slid into the booth. "I'll pay you back as soon as I find my purse."

"Don't worry about it. I know Wila would have done the same thing for my grandmother." Francine glanced at Laura who shook her head. Well, maybe it was best to explain everything once they got to Wila's house.

Mrs. Wilkinson bit into the egg, bacon, and cheese sandwich and made yummy noises as she chewed. After she swallowed, she turned to Laura. "Are you related to the Penny girl who owns this coffee shop?"

Laura smiled. "She's my daughter-in-law."

Mrs. Wilkinson chuckled. "I'm not a fan of the fancy coffee she serves, but her sandwiches are excellent. Your granddaughter's the same age as my great-grandson. Never saw a baby girl with such bright red hair. And Penny was such a help to Wila in finding a daycare."

"They've been friends for quite a while," Laura said.

Mrs. Wilkinson cocked her head and stared at Laura. "It's only been six months."

Oh, crap. Laura froze as she realized her mistake.

Francine forced a laugh. "My Brittany's the same age as Justine and Derek. It feels like forever when you're sleep-deprived."

"It's been a few decades, but I still remember how exhausted I was," Laura added.

Mrs. Wilkinson chuckled and nodded. "Between working two jobs and bearing six children, exhaustion was my daily life, but my kids were worth every minute."

She and Laura clinked cups.

Francine relaxed a bit. All she had to do was get Mrs. Wilkinson over to Wila's.

Easy, right?

Chapter 12

A half hour later, Francine drove her friends' resurrected family members to the super store. She grimaced while Mrs. Wilkinson continued her rant.

"What size do I wear?" From the front passenger seat, Mrs. Wilkinson shook her right index finger at Francine. "What are they teaching you girls these days? Asking such personal questions of people you've just met?"

A rumble vibrated beneath Francine's thighs. Great. Now her minivan/horse was offended on her behalf.

"Mrs. Wilkinson, I'm trying to help," Francine said as gently as she could. "First of all, Wila is on the night shift this week, and I woke her up. Second, the clothes you're wearing have been damaged and need to be cleaned. Third, I'm sure you will want to take a shower, and Wila doesn't have any of your clothes at her house—"

"House? What house?" At least, the confusion stopped Mrs. Wilkinson from shaking her finger in Francine's face. "When did she and Deion move out of their apartment?"

Laura leaned over the console between the two front seats. "I think we need to take her straight to Wila's place, instead of stopping at the store."

"But she needs something to wear." Francine flipped on the right turn signal and tapped the brakes for the upcoming entrance to the shopping center parking lot.

"Don't be talking about me like I'm not here," Mrs. Wilkinson scolded. "I won't put up with being ignored. I marched for our rights—"

"I'm sorry for insulting you, ma'am." The super store idea was efficient, but it wasn't what Mrs. Wilkinson needed. Francine swallowed a grimace. She really was turning into Penny.

She switched off the turn signal and whipped her minivan out of the turn lane and back into the thru-lane. "You're right, Mrs. Wilkinson. I'm going to take you to Wila because you need to be with family when you hear the truth."

When Francine pulled into Wila's driveway a few minutes later, Mrs. Wilkinson stared at the house. "How on earth can Wila and Deion afford a place like this?"

Ignoring the question, Francine shifted the gear into park and switched off the engine. "Wila's expecting us. You can ask her all the personal questions you want."

Mrs. Wilkinson shot her a dirty look, but at least, she didn't start on another tirade.

All three women got out of the minivan and walked up the stone path to the portico. When Francine raised her fist to knock, Wila yanked open the front door, her attention fixed on Mrs. Wilkinson.

"Gammy?" Wila's voice hoarsened. "Is it really you?"

"Course it is, girl," Mrs. Wilkinson blurted. "Why are you looking at me like I just walked out of my grave?"

Wila pushed past Francine and seized her grandmother in a tight hug, laughing and crying at the same time.

Francine glanced around and caught one of Wila's neighbors watching them. "Can we continue the reunion inside, ladies?"

Wila sniffed and nodded. "Let's go in. I started a pot of coffee for us."

They followed Wila into her house. As Francine shut the front door, Mrs. Wilkinson stopped in the middle of the living room.

"I don't remember this place." Mrs. Wilkinson looked around at the furniture and pictures on the wall. "When did you and Deion move in here?"

"Deion's never lived here, Gammy." Wila hugged herself.

"Maybe I should wait in the car," Laura whispered in Francine's ear.

"No," Francine whispered back. "I have a feeling we're going to need your help in a couple of minutes."

"You two split up, and you didn't tell me?" Mrs. Wilkinson stared at Wila with an appalled expression. "When did this happen?" The elderly woman pointed at one of the photos on the wall. "And who's that boy in the picture with you?"

"That's Derek, Gammy."

"No." Mrs. Wilkinson shook her head in total denial. "No. He's just started walking. That boy—" She stared at the picture.

"Derek's twelve now," Wila said. "The reason you don't know that is because you had a stroke in your sleep eleven years ago."

"If I had a stroke, where have I been? Why am I in my good dress from your wedding? Why—" She appeared thunderstruck and started to collapse. Francine and Wila caught her before she hit the carpet and helped her to the couch.

Once Mrs. Wilkinson was settled, Francine said, "I'll get her a bottle of water."

When she returned from the kitchen with the drink, Laura sat next to the older woman and held her left hand.

"—same thing happened to me this morning. You and I aren't the only ones who have risen from the grave."

"I-I can't believe I've been dead these last eleven years." Mrs. Wilkinson shook her head before she looked at Wila. "Is that why you didn't want to talk to me on Francine's phone?"

"I'm sorry, Gammy." Wila had the grace to look embarrassed. "I already ran into a couple of other dead people today. I didn't want to believe you were back. I-I can't handle losing you again."

"Oh, baby." Mrs. Wilkinson grabbed Wila, and they both burst into tears.

Francine set the water bottle on the end table by Wila. "Why don't Laura and I get that change of clothes while you two talk? Do you need me to pick up any groceries for you, Wila?"

Wila and her grandmother parted, and they both sniffed and wiped at their faces.

"No, thank you. We're set on food." Wila chuckled. "I'd planned on tacos tonight, but I heard you stuffed all the kids with them this afternoon."

Francine grinned. "I'm taking advantage of being able to eat anything I want, but I didn't mean to ruin your dinner plans."

"As for the clothes, Gammy wears extra-large—" Wila started.

"Girl, don't you be telling your friends that kind of stuff!" Mrs. Wilkinson protested.

"Gammy, all of your clothes went to the church donation drive. I'm not trying to be mean or contrary. As much as I love you, you're not going to fit into any of my outfits."

Mrs. Wilkinson harrumphed.

Wila finished giving Francine her grandmother's sizes, which she scribbled on the notepad she kept in her tote.

"We'll be back soon." Francine slid her notebook and pen back in their special pocket.

"Wait." Wila glanced at her grandmother. "Should I go to Penny's and get Derek? He was supposed to spend the night at Dani's house, but if she's too, um, busy with family stuff . . ."

"I don't know what our exact plan will be yet." Francine forced a smile. "We were trying to let you get some sleep since you're on shift tonight. One of us may be hosting a slumber party if that's all right."

Wila's shoulders relaxed. "That would be awesome. I owe you guys one."

"Oh, please." Francine waved a dismissive hand. "You've done enough errand running for the rest of us on your days off. Your karma is balanced."

Francine and Laura exited the house and climbed back into the black minivan.

"It's good you girls have each other to rely on," Laura murmured.

Francine pushed the ignition button. "You didn't have any mom friends when Gene and Theo were kids?"

"None that I trusted." Laura made a face. "A good chunk of the mothers on our street were divorcees. A larger percentage of them as well as a number of married women tried to seduce Ed over the years."

"Edward?" Francine glanced at Laura before she started backing out of Wila's drive. "Why? No offense, but he's . . ." No word that wouldn't be an insult popped into her mind.

"A stick-in-the-mud?" Laura volunteered. "Male chauvinist pig? Asshole?"

Francine shifted her minivan into drive and pressed the accelerator. "The phrase I was searching for was 'rigidly conservative.'"

Laura laughed. "Regardless, it's nice you have girlfriends you trust. Like Wila."

Francine laughed in return. "Normally, Wila and I are at each other's throats. My white privilege and her childhood on the Chicago streets don't exactly mesh."

"Does any of that matter now with what you've become?" Laura asked.

"No," Francine replied. "No, it doesn't."

Chapter 13

After dropping off new clothes and shoes for Mrs. Wilkinson, Francine phoned Penny through her hands-free app as she drove out of Wila's subdivision.

"How's things going at Casa Hudson?"

"Edward hid in his room until Marian left." The disgust over her father-in-law's lack of integrity when confronted with both his wife and his girlfriend was evident in Penny's voice. "He's now in the family room, regaling Gene, Dani, and the kids with stories about his and Laura's demon hunting days."

Francine laughed. "That's better than my afternoon."

"Oh, god." Penny groaned. "Did you and Wila get into another fight?"

"No, it was her grandmother who threw the hissy fit this time, so I had to take her to Wila's house before I could get her some clothes."

"You two did tell her the truth, didn't you?" Penny asked.

"She kind of figured it out before we actually blurted the words." Francine glanced at Laura. "Your mother-in-law was a big help with Mrs. Wilkinson."

"It was the difference between me dying two years ago versus her eleven," Laura said dryly. "Wila had moved and divorced, and Derek was no longer the baby Latricia remembered."

"Can you handle the circus at your house?" Francine asked. "Wila was worried because Derek was supposed to spend the night at Dani's."

"We've got couches, blankets, and plenty of food." Penny laughed.

"Though Edward threatened to force-feed tranquilizers to Dani if she stayed here past Monday."

"Crap," Francine muttered.

"Don't worry. The kids pointed out he shouldn't be messing with Death."

"And where is Marian staying?" Laura blurted.

"Marian went home, and Ed's staying here." Penny's sigh whistled through the receiver. "Honestly, Laura, you two could have been good friends if the circumstances were different."

"I hope you'll remember that when another woman waltzes into your home and kisses Gene." The expression on Laura's face didn't bode well for the next time she saw either Edward or Marian.

Francine bit her lip to keep from saying that marital vows said, "Until death do you part." They didn't say a damn thing about what happens if one spouse rises from the grave. Though if another woman came into her home like the interloper owned the place, she'd be feeling as homicidal as Laura was right now.

"Please, Laura, I don't want to fight with you or anyone else." Penny sounded on the verge of tears. "This situation is difficult for all of us."

Francine gritted her teeth. Time to change the subject. "Tell Dani we'll drive by her place and make sure everything's okay."

"I'll tell her." The only reason Penny didn't have her phone on speaker was the kids. Well, maybe Edward and Gene, too. "We'll talk to you later."

Francine disconnected the call and eyed Laura. "Would it bother you if we swing by Oakfield Cemetery after we check Dani's house? It's going to be dark soon, and I don't want to be falling into someone's empty grave."

The older woman nodded. "Someone needs to get a handle on the situation, and local law enforcement won't have a clue."

Francine found herself wishing Laura Hudson hadn't died two years ago. The Soccer Moms of the Apocalypse could have used someone with her knowledge when their abilities started manifesting earlier this month.

After a thorough examination, there was no evidence of anyone, much less Dani's deceased husband, around her house. Francine used her spare key to double-check the interior. She and Laura agreed there was no sense wasting any more time here, climbed back into Sable, and headed to the Oakfield Cemetery.

The bottom edge of the sun touched the horizon when they approached the main entrance of the town's largest graveyard. Vehicles lined the berms of the street that ran along the southern border. Even more bothersome was the number of men and women with rifles who lined the wrought-iron fence. The thirty or so armed people focused on the cemetery itself.

Francine tried to turn into the entrance, only to find the road blocked by two pickups, a tan one and a scarlet one with wide gray stripes along the sides and bed. The main gate was pulled shut, and the chains were wrapped around the bars, though it didn't look to be padlocked. A man approached the driver side of Sable and motioned for Francine to roll down the window. Like a lot of the others lining the fence, he wore jeans, boots, and a hunting jacket. However, the logo of Chicago's major league football team emblazoned his baseball cap.

He ducked his head to face Francine. "You ladies need to turn around and go home."

"The Oakfield Cemetery is open to the public during daylight hours." Francine glared at the man.

"Maybe you haven't heard, but there's dead people coming out of that cemetery. I don't want to see you ladies get your brains eaten—"

"Hank! We got one!"

Hank must have been the guy trying to warn Francine. He backed up a couple of paces and yelled, "Where?"

"Over by the Dorchester section." A man stood in the bed of a raised, electric blue pickup on her right. He held a pair of binoculars to his face. Hank jogged over to join his friend.

Francine opened her van door and slipped out. Laura followed suit. The vigilantes' attention was focused on the cherub statue on a tall pedestal four rows into the cemetery.

No, not on the statue. On the heaving dirt at the monument's base.

Shit. Rose Dorchester, the daughter of one of Oakfield's founders, was buried there. A little girl who'd died of smallpox. Brittany had to do a paper on what it was like living in the town two centuries ago, which is why the little factoid stuck in Francine's brain.

She charged for the gate. Shouting from Hank and a couple of others followed. One of the men managed to get a hand on her, but she shook it off and shoved the gate open. That poor little girl had died horribly once before. She couldn't let that happen again.

A small hand burst from the dormant grass and damp earth as Francine raced for the grave. She dropped to her knees and started digging with her bare hands.

Someone knelt on the other side of the child's hand. Laura furiously scooped damp top soil away from the mud-streaked white flesh. Another small arm appeared.

"Hold on!" Francine yelled. "We're getting you out."

The top of her head appeared.

Laura thrust her arm into the soil. "I've got her beneath a shoulder. Can you get the other one?"

Francine dug a little more. If she didn't get herself shot today, she was definitely getting that mani pedi tomorrow. Her now filthy hands found the girl's other shoulder joint.

"Got her!"

Together, she and Laura worked the tiny body free from the grave. The little girl's white burial dress was ruined, partly through age and partly through the efforts of escaping from her coffin. Laura pulled the girl into her lap.

The child plucked at her dress. "Mama is going to be so mad I got mud on my dress."

Francine and Laura exchanged looks before they both cracked up laughing.

"Sweetie, given the circumstances, I think your mother will understand—"

"Get away from that thing!"

Francine looked up to find Hank, a woman, and three other men standing nearby, guns aimed at the little girl, and subsequently Laura. This was not going to end well if someone didn't talk them down. Francine climbed to her feet.

"Do what the police and sheriff's departments recommend," she said. "Go home and lock your doors."

"We're not going to let these zombies take over our town," Hank snapped.

"No one's taking over anything." Francine stepped between the people with guns and the two resurrected people behind her.

"I'm a God-fearing Christian," the woman yelled. "This is unnatural."

"Is it really?" Francine asked. "Don't you read the Scriptures? Do you know what the rising of the dead means?"

Two of the men exchanged worried looks, but Ed and the other two people didn't look as convinced.

"Have any of you checked the graves of your loved ones?" Francine added. "How would you feel if your parents or siblings came back and someone shot them because they were afraid?"

A wail rose and fell in the distance. She prayed someone had the common sense to call 9-1-1 when they saw these people lined up along the fence.

"Drop your weapons," another woman said.

The five armed idiots shifted to point their barrels at someone behind Francine. She looked over her shoulder.

A woman approached them. She dressed similarly to everyone else. Blue jeans, steel-toed boots, and a wool-lined denim jacket. And like everyone else, she had a gun, except hers was a handgun, not a rifle. Unlike everyone else, her hair was dyed an electric blue that glinted under the last of the weak October sunshine.

Behind the new woman, dirty faces peered around the trunks of the naked maples in the memorial glen.

"There's five of us," Hank boasted.

"Who probably can't hit the broadside of a barn," the blue-haired lady retorted.

"How about we all lower our guns before someone gets hurt while we figure things out?" Francine's heart pounded. It was getting harder to keep Famine on her leash with everyone's tension.

"I'm not getting my brains eaten because some bitch with crazy hair said so," the woman on Hank's side said.

"No one's brains have been eaten." Francine held up her hands. "I swear."

"Yeah, and you Astins probably built a bunker with all your money," the rifle woman sneered. "You'll leave the rest of us to rot."

Of course, she recognized Francine. The TV ads had made her nearly as recognizable in the area as Neal.

The rifle woman's face contorted with fear and anger, but it didn't have the bubbling and shifting effect of demon possession. None of the six people with guns did. Nope, humans could be stupid in their own right without demon assistance.

"I understand you're scared," Francine said. "One of my best friends had her dead mother-in-law show up on her doorstep. I ran into another friend's dead grandmother at a coffee shop. And a third friend who's a widow is panicked as hell that her dead husband will show up and scare her son.

"But I'll say it again, these are our loved ones. From my encounters so far, they are as scared and confused as we are. Shooting each other isn't going to help. We need some patience and understanding while we figure this thing out."

The sirens were getting closer. All she needed to do was stall until the police arrived.

Unless the cops took Hank and his friends' side.

It didn't help she could practically taste everyone's fear, including the recently risen hiding in the grove fifty yards away. The problem was their fear tasted better than the Long Johns she'd eaten this morning.

"You saying the dead are rising like the prophets' foretold in Zechariah and Revelation?" the first worried man said.

"Yes," Francine said. "And my guess is how we treat the resurrected determines what happens next."

"Kill 'em all and let God sort them out," Hank's fourth buddy said.

"Ma'am, you, your friend, and the girl need to take cover." The blue-haired woman was now standing beside Francine. "I don't think these guys are going to listen to you."

"You can't shoot them," she whispered. "They're just scared."

"And I've seen scared people do a lot of stupid shit," the woman said.

"I'm going to distract them," Francine said. "Get everyone to safety if you can."

"What are you two bitches whispering about?" the one who wanted to kill everyone demanded.

"Scripture." Francine side-stepped away from Laura and Rose.

"Wait a minute. The Four Horsemen are supposed to come before the dead rise," the second man with a worried expression protested.

"You're right." Francine let her alter ego slip free. "And we're already here."

Chapter 14

Hank and his friends made some pretty spectacular high-pitched screeches. The man who advocated shooting everyone dropped his rifle before he ran for the cemetery gate. The blue-haired woman didn't bat an eyelash though and kept her weapon trained on the four wannabe vigilantes who remained. Laura had been paying attention and dragged little Rose Dorchester behind her family's mausoleum when Francine let Famine out to play.

She couldn't stop the burble of laughter that erupted from her now emaciated chest. Fear had never been an emotion she inspired in people, but it was so damn delicious.

"Don't hurt us." The man who mentioned the Four Horsemen slowly knelt before he laid his rifle on the dormant grass and raised his hands.

"Do you know who I am?" she asked.

It was the female vigilante who answered. "Y-you're Neal Astin's wife."

The kneeling man bowed his head. "You're Famine."

"Good. You understand." Maybe her bluff would work after all. "I don't want to hurt you. Any of you. But I can't allow you to harm the rising dead either. It's supper time. Go home. Cook your meals. And thank the Creator you can feed your children."

Tires squealed out on the street, and people were shouting. Damn, she needed to get Famine under control before the police saw her.

"Go," she repeated.

Hank and his two standing buddies whirled and ran for it. The kneeling man rose. He picked up his rifle before he inclined his head. "Thank you for going easy on us."

"I didn't want you to hurt someone. And please take your friend's weapon so somebody doesn't harm themselves with it."

He nodded and gathered the other gun before he followed his companions though his pace was far more leisurely. Hopefully, she given him something to think about.

"You'd better hope no one caught your little transformation on camera." The blue-haired woman lowered her arms. She watched the crowd a few more seconds before she placed her weapon in her back waistband holster. "And you've got about ten seconds to turn human again before the cops see you."

"Speaking of which, Illinois isn't an open carry state." Francine closed her eyes and tugged on the memory of her parents taking her and her brother to Disneyworld. She really needed to give Evan a call tonight to make sure his family plus Mom and Dad were doing okay.

"Then it's a good thing I've got my concealed carry permit," the blue-haired woman said dryly. "The way you change is cool and freaky at the same time."

Francine opened her eyes. "My husband has the same opinion."

The blue-haired woman held out her right hand. "Karen Longstreet, Vatican taskforce."

"Francine Coy-Astin, Famine of the Soccer Moms of the Apocalypse."

"Soccer Moms?" Karen's eyebrow, dyed to match her hair, rose.

"We aren't exactly men, all of our kids belong to the same soccer team, and we drive minivans." Francine shook Karen's hand before she waved at the mausoleum. "My friend back there is Laura Hudson."

Karen's eyes widened. "*The* Laura Hudson?"

Penny's mother-in-law peered around the edge of the small marble building. "No, just Laura."

Karen grinned. "Well, Just Laura, you and your husband are freakin' legends in the taskforce. It's an honor to meet you in the flesh."

"Can I go home?" Little Rose Dorchester stepped around Laura. "Mama and Papa will be cross with me for being out after dark."

Twilight had fallen during the stand-off. Movement caught Francine's attention. The people from the grove carefully approached her little group.

Like Laura and Mrs. Wilkinson earlier, all of them had mud smeared on their clothes and soil clinging to their skin and hair. The clothing they wore ranged from Rose's time period to the present day. The small grace was none of the others were children. But they all needed help.

Francine bit her lip. She couldn't take the entire group home. Their house was pretty good-sized, but she couldn't handle all of them.

Flashlight beams swept over the group. She turned to find at least six of Oakfield's finest approaching them. Her heart sank. One of the officers was Miles Pence who already suspected Penny was behind the death of Seth Rimmon, the developer possessed by a demon.

"Don't say a word," Francine hissed. "Let me handle this."

"Don't you ladies know there's a curfew in effect?" Pence snapped.

"No, sir. We didn't." Francine gestured at the group of newly risen. "We were just trying to help these people."

Pence flashed his light in her face. "Well, if it isn't Mrs. Neal Astin. What kind of trouble are you and your fellow soccer moms causing this time?" Damn, he was worse than the mean girls on her high school cheer squad.

She lifted her chin. "As I said before, it's Ms. Coy-Astin, and neither Karen or Laura are soccer moms."

"Had to recruit new friends so you don't land in jail with Penny Hudson?" Pence scoffed.

"My husband planned to donate funds to the Oakfield first responders to replace the money promised by a two-bit con artist," Francine said coolly. "If you're still taking said con artist's side over the woman he was harassing, I have to wonder why."

The other officers all looked at Pence.

For once, Francine enjoyed the ability to see in the dark, one of the gifts being a Soccer Mom of the Apocalypse afforded her. No one else could detect the fierce blush on Pence's lily white cheeks.

"We need to see IDs before you three can leave," Pence demanded. "The rest of you folks who came out of your graves will have to come to the police station."

"Don't let that horrible man take me, Miss Laura," Rose wailed.

"You don't have a say."

Francine began to understand how stress triggered Penny's migraines and why she disliked Pence so much. "Officer, she's scared, and she doesn't understand what's happened to her."

"You have no authority—"

"Chill, Miles," his partner Simmons hissed.

Francine squelched the urge to laugh at the delicious odor of fear coming from the other officers. Simmons and the rest were nervous at being in a cemetery after dark with a bunch of dead people. They certainly wouldn't take such a response from her very well.

"I'll be responsible for Rose Dorchester," she said. "Have CPS come to my home tomorrow if you have a problem with that. But my guess is you'll have your hands full. This isn't the only cemetery in the city limits."

"Where are you taking the other people?" Laura demanded.

"That's none of your business." Pence's behavior went beyond unpleasant.

"It is if the police department starts a house-to-house for people whose only crime is coming back from the dead." Francine waved at the frightened group huddled together. "They need help. Food, a shower, and some clean clothes. Not jail."

Another officer stepped between Pence and Francine. He appeared to be close to her age, and he would have been cute if not for the cheesy, thick upper lip hair.

"Ma'am, we're taking them to the high school. The Red Cross has set up an emergency shelter in the gymnasium."

"What help do you need there, Officer . . ."

He took the hint. "Officer Rick Graham, Ms. Coy-Astin. Like you said, we need food, personal toiletries, clothes, and blankets. We are trying to get these people off the streets. Already had a couple of these type of folks admitted to the hospital with injuries."

"What time does curfew end?"

"Dawn," he replied.

"This isn't something you can just throw money at," Pence sneered.

Francine chose to ignore him. "I'll start the phone tree. Between the Oakfield Parents Association and the religious organizations, we should have supplies for you by morning."

"That would be appreciated, Ms. Coy-Astin." Officer Graham bobbed his head. "I'll let Sergeant Park know to expect you."

"Thank you." She bestowed him with her best pageant smile. "Laura, Karen, let's get Rose home. We'll see the rest of you in the morning."

While Francine and her little group walked toward the gates of the cemetery, she chewed on her bottom lip. Why did she have the terrible feeling this was only the tip of the undead iceberg?

Chapter 15

Francine waited at the end of the street for Karen. Laura sat in the back and held Rose. The little girl was still hysterical about Pence's threat to put her in jail. The fact that Francine didn't have horses pulling her minivan didn't register with the child.

A sports car roared up to the corner. The headlights flashed in the pattern Francine and Laura agreed to, and Francine flashed her lights in return. She shifted the gear into drive and accelerated down Baxter. Karen turned left and followed her minivan.

It was time to double-check the self-claimed demon hunter's story. Francine tapped the controls on the steering wheel to call Father Perez.

"Saint Michael's Catholic Church."

"Good evening, Father. I need to ask something." She sucked in a deep breath. "Did Father McAvoy call in anyone from the Vatican taskforce?"

"I know he's called in several favors to get a team here." Muffled men's voices rumbled in the background before Father Perez said, "The only demon hunter who might already be in Oakfield is a lady named Karen Longstreet. She was supposed to drive up from Springfield—"

He laughed.

"What?" Francine demanded.

"She's on Father McAvoy's cell phone right now, saying she ran into Famine and the illustrious Laura Hudson at the Oakfield Cemetery."

Francine breathed a sigh of relief. "Thanks, I just wanted to confirm her identity before I offer her a bed at my house."

"It sounds like you have enough on your hands," Father Perez said. "Father McAvoy told her we have a room for her at the rectory."

"No offense, Father, but I want her at my house. It's been a very long, very weird day. Karen didn't freak out when she saw my alter ego, and I'd like to have some backup at home. My sisters have their hands full with their own problems at the moment."

"All right," the padre conceded. "Call me if you need anything tonight."

"There's a curfew, Father. It's better if you don't get arrested."

They said their goodbyes, and Francine disconnected the call.

"It would be nice to see Deke again," Laura murmured from the back seat.

"At some point this weekend, we can have a get together at our place," Francine responded. "That's assuming we don't accidentally destroy the world before Monday."

"How are we moving without horses?" Rose shrieked.

Yep, it was going to be a very long weekend.

While Laura helped Rose with the intricacies of a modern bathroom, Francine dumped a bag of Brittany's outgrown clothes that hadn't made it to the donation center yet on her daughter's bed. Bless her heart, Karen helped sort through the pile.

"I take it you knew who and what I was before we met," Francine said.

"Father McAvoy filled me in on the drive here." Karen checked the size on a pair of leggings. "Don't worry. He's the team lead on this situation, and he's treating everything on a need-to-know basis. He didn't want me to freak out if I ran into one of the Soccer Moms of the Apocalypse."

She snickered. "By the way, that's a way cooler name than the Four Horsemen. Who came up with that?"

"Wila, our resident queen of snark." Francine set aside a couple of shirts that would fit Rose. "Did the father call in an entire team?"

"Just me so far." Karen added a pair of jeans to the wearable pile and tossed another back into the plastic bag. "I'm from Springfield and was home on leave visiting my sister and her family." She shrugged. "I was the closest taskforce member to you. If we need to, I can call my team leader Sister Mary Teresa. She lives in Ohio. But if you have the Hudsons and Father McAvoy here already, you're gold. Their team is a fucking legend!"

Francine paused in her sorting. "Karen, I don't mean to be a prude, but watch the swearing. Rose is having a hard enough time, and women of her era didn't say things like that. At least, not in public."

"Sorry." Karen shot her a rueful grin. "I'll do my best to watch my words."

"Francine!" Neal's voice echoed up the stairwell.

"I'm in Brittany's room!"

Soft thumping on the steps preceded her husband in the doorway. "Hey, babe! How'd the rest of your day—" He stepped into the room and stared at Karen. "I don't remember Gene's mom ever having blue hair."

"This is Karen Longstreet." Francine smiled. "She's with the Vatican taskforce. Father McAvoy is calling in some favors. I told her she could stay here."

Neal grinned. "Now you know where Brittany gets it from."

Francine stopped in mid-fold with a pair of cotton twill pants. "Where she gets what?"

"The urge to rescue every stray in the neighborhood."

She laughed. "The Waltons' purebred cocker spaniel was not a stray. Neither was Mr. Fulton's Yorkie."

"Technically, I am an American mutt," Karen said. "But I am here on purpose."

Francine finished folding the pants. Too bad, the demon hunter was only here temporarily. She would fit in nicely with her friends.

Her real friends. Even before they became the Soccer Moms of the Apocalypse, Penny, Wila, and Dani were the first women Francine really felt comfortable enough to expose the aspects of herself that were inconvenient or unwanted by others.

She'd played the stay-at-home-mom game to keep the town bitches and their daughters from taking their displeasure out on Brittany. She didn't for one minute regret staying home and spending time with her daughter. But it took Brittany standing up for herself when she wanted to play sports instead of becoming an online influencer like most of the other preteen girls for Francine to realize in protecting Brittany, she was holding her daughter back.

Just like her own mother did in an effort to protect Francine.

The only other person, besides the other Soccer Moms, who saw all her facets was Neal.

"Bath accomplished," Laura said cheerily as she guided Rose, wrapped in a bath sheet, into Brittany's bedroom from the connecting bathroom.

The little girl took one look at Neal, shrieked, and darted back into the bathroom. The door slammed shut, rattling Brittany's crystal menagerie on their shelf.

Neal looked at Francine askance. "I think there's a visitor you forgot to mention."

"That was Rose Dorchester."

"*The* Rose Dorchester?" Neal's eyebrows rose. "As in 'kiss the cherub watching over her grave for good luck' Rose Dorchester?"

"Yeah." Francine winced. She'd forgotten about that local legend. "I couldn't let Child Protective Services take her. At least, Laura and Mrs. Wilkinson have some clue about twenty-first century life. Rose is two hundred years out of time.

Neal scratched the back of his head. "That explains the crazy guy claiming to be Jebediah Hauser this morning."

"You saw him?" Francine asked.

"Yeah." He wore a bemused expression. "We could hear him yelling during our breakfast meeting at the Main Street Bistro. That was quickly followed by the police chasing the poor guy all over downtown. Good grief, can you imagine getting tased and not knowing what the heck was happening to you?"

"Speaking of not knowing what's happening to you, get out, Neal." Laura glared at him. "We've got an eight-year-old child who's already freaked out enough."

"Sorry." Neal held up his hands. "With the crazy day, I totally forgot to place an order with The Steak House. I'll go do that now."

"That would be awesome." Francine smiled. "An extra meal for me?"

"Whatever my lady desires."

"What about the city curfew?" Karen asked.

"We've got until eight p.m. according to the emergency bulletin," Neal said.

"Get out, Neal," Laura repeated with a glare.

Francine stepped closer to her husband. "Go before the demon hunter gets really angry." Her stomach growled as she pecked him on the lips.

"Ah, crap." He winced. "I'm so sorry, babe." Yep, he understood her all too well. Every time she let Famine out to play, the transformation literally left her starving.

Neal pulled the door shut behind him.

Laura knocked on the bathroom door. "Rose, honey, it's safe to come out now."

"No."

From the choked word, Francine suspected poor little Rose had hit her breaking point. The minivan ride to the Astin house had been bad enough, but Sable got pissy when Francine tried to explain horseless carriages to the child and threatened to stall out halfway home.

She crossed to the bedroom door. "Rose, I have some of my daughter's clothes for you to wear. It's just us ladies. My husband Neal went to get us some dinner."

The bathroom door opened, but just a wide enough sliver Francine could see a big blue eye staring up at her. "You mean he's ordering the cook and maid to bring us dinner? Papa says a real man doesn't do women's work."

Francine crouched in front of the door. "Things are a lot different than you last remember. It's not only horseless carriages and hot water piped through the walls. But we still dress properly for a meal."

The door opened wider. "But you and Miss Laura and Miss Karen dress like men," Rose whispered.

"These days we wear what's comfortable." Francine shrugged. "That means men wear skirts and women wear pants. If that's what they want. Otherwise, we all still cover our private bits in polite company."

Rose giggled. "It would be very funny if Papa wore one of Mama's dresses."

"Well, that would only work if they were the same size." Laura grinned. "We would have to buy a larger size for my husband Edward."

"Are you rich?" Rose's eyes widened.

"No, sweetie." Laura's face scrunched with her confusion. "Why?"

"Even Mama and Mrs. Butler, our housekeeper, make most of our clothes. Papa says buying clothes is a waste of money, but there are some things Mama and Mrs. Butler can't make, like boots and hats."

"Francine! Get down here!"

She jumped at the panic in Neal's voice. What was going on? The last time he sounded that freaked was when her water broke at the country club. She twisted the lever, yanked open the bedroom door, and raced for the stairs.

"Back in the bathroom, Rose," Laura hissed behind Francine.

Footsteps thundered in her wake as she ran down the stairs. Neal sat on one of the barstools at the breakfast counter, staring at the TV. One of the Chicago stations broadcasted the local news. And on screen . . .

Shaky amateur footage showed Francine confronting Ed and his little group of vigilantes by Rose's grave.

And worse, her transformation into Famine.

Chapter 16

"Oh, my God." Francine let her head fall into her palms. So much for trying to make life easier for her friends. She'd just outed them to the world.

"Well, shit," Karen muttered. "I thought you had demons in the house. Which, by the way, I can put up warding sigils for you."

Francine looked up in time to see Karen once again holster her gun. Laura stood behind the current taskforce member, one of Neal's nine irons in her hands.

On the TV, the perky blond anchor smirked into the camera. "While the woman in the photo appears to be Francine Astin, wife of metro area car magnate Neal Astin, calls to the Astin Auto main office have yet to be returned."

Francine turned to her husband. "Neal, I'm so, so sorry. Those idiots with guns were going to shoot a child—"

"I'm not pissed at you, babe." His sharp-planed jaw had softened a bit from when they were in high school. But he had the same look of determination he had when he got knocked down on the football field or when someone tried to mess with his business.

Which whoever had given the TV station that video had just done.

"You need call the other Soccer Moms while I pick up dinner." Neal stood and shoved his phone in the front pocket of his slacks.

Guilt smacked Francine. The poor guy hadn't had a chance to change his clothes, and he'd been going since five this morning.

"Why don't you stay here and relax—" she began.

"No." Neal exhaled gustily. "Let me help you for once, babe. Close all the blinds and drapes. Lock the doors and set the security system. Tell Sable to stay cool and not leave the garage."

"Maybe you shouldn't go." Francine bit her lower lip.

"I've already paid for the food." He pulled her close and kissed her. "I promise I'll go straight to The Steak House and right back. Call them." He headed for the garage.

For the first time, she understood why Neal insisted on buying a house in a gated community. Security wouldn't let the reporters in. It didn't mean news crews weren't camped outside the gates.

And he'd be driving right into the middle of them.

"He can take care of himself." Karen rested a hand on her shoulder. "You need to warn your sisters."

Francine slumped against the breakfast bar. "How did this go so wrong?"

Laura set the nine iron against the pantry door. "It hasn't gone wrong yet. But Karen's right, you need to call Penny and Wila. Let them know what's going on. Dani hasn't changed her mind about spending the night at Gene and Penny's, has she?"

The two demon hunters were only making sense. Francine chewed on her lower lip. So much for trying to prove she could take care of her friends.

"I'd better make sure." She pulled her phone out of her pocket and pressed the speed dial for Penny. It rang three times when Penny breathlessly answered, "Hey, Francine! Have you seen the news?"

"That's what I was calling you about." She winced. "I'm so, so sorry. I never meant—"

"It was a matter of time." Penny sighed. "Let me put you on speaker so Dani can join the conversation." There was a beep.

"What are you trying to do?" Dani screeched. "Put up a sign for all the demons saying here's where you can find the Four Horsemen!"

Francine's phone beeped, and she checked the screen. "Just a second.

Wila's calling me. Let me conference her in so you can all yell at me at the same time."

She pressed the appropriate controls.

"What the ever-loving fuck, Francine!" Wila yelled.

"Hey, watch the language!" Penny snapped. "We have children in the house, and Dani and I are on speaker."

"So do we," Laura said. "Speaking of which, I'll go back upstairs and take care of Rose."

"Who's Rose?" Penny asked.

"Rose Dorchester," Karen said.

"The daughter of Ebenezer Dorchester, one of the founders of Oakfield," Francine said. "Some very frightened people with guns were taking potshots at the folks rising out of their graves. I couldn't let them shoot a little girl who has no clue of what is happening to her. That's how I got filmed."

"Oh, my god," Penny whispered.

"I'm sorry for yelling at you," Dani said. "You couldn't let them hurt her."

"That could have been Gammy." Wila audibly gulped. "I'm sorry for yelling at you, too."

"I'm glad you're all repentant." Francine crossed to the built in desk and pulled open the top drawer. "We need to activate the Parents Association phone tree. The police are housing the risen dead at the high school gym for now, but they need supplies."

"You do know the entire county is under a curfew, right?" Wila said.

"Yes, but it ends at dawn." Francine repeated the list of things Officer Graham has requested. "Dani, can you call Father Perez and see what help Saint Michael's can give?" With the chaos at the cemetery, Francine had forgotten to mention the police's needs when she spoke with the priest.

"Yes."

"I'll call Reverend Sanford, too," Wila volunteered.

"Thanks," Francine said. "How's your grandmother doing?"

"She's upstairs taking a shower," Wila answered. "Thanks again for picking up some clothes for her."

"Once we get the supplies to the high school tomorrow, we'll meet at Java's Palace and try to figure out a plan." Francine glanced at Karen. "And just to let you know, Father McAvoy called in another demon hunter from the Vatican taskforce to help us. Her name's Karen Longstreet."

"I'm assuming she's the blue-haired woman with you and Laura in the video," Dani said.

"Yes," Francine answered as Karen called out, "Hi, ladies!"

"Sounds like a plan, Francine," Penny said. "Let us get started on the phone calls for supplies, and we'll see the rest of you in the morning."

Everyone hung up, and Francine tapped the end call icon on her own phone. She looked at Karen. "Do you know how insane our lives have become when not one of them questioned your inclusion in our meeting tomorrow?"

Karen laughed. "Actually, it's nice meeting people who don't look at me like I'm crazy when I tell them what I do for a living."

"I don't consider the Horsemen thing as my job."

"You're right. In your case, it's a literal calling."

Francine sighed. "I need the bumper sticker that says God doesn't give us more than we can handle, but I wish he didn't trust me so much."

"Why do I have a feeling the folks in this neighbor will go absolutely apeshit if you dared to put a bumper sticker on your minivan?" Karen grinned.

"I think Sable would be more irritated with me."

"Your husband mentioned her before. Who is she?" Karen asked.

"Instead of a robot, my minivan turns into a horse."

Chapter 17

Francine waited while Karen took a few seconds for that concept to work its way through her brain.

"Your minivan is your horse?" the demon hunter said.

"Yes, just don't ask me how it works." Francine held up her hands. "They may not be able to speak, but we can sense what each of our horses is thinking and feeling. Their horse form manifests when we need them. Otherwise, they are the minivans we each bought over the last ten months."

Her stomach grumbled. She wasn't going to make it until Neal got back with dinner. Thank goodness, she bought an extra deli roasted chicken yesterday at the grocery store. She retrieved the chicken and the bottle of mayonnaise from the refrigerator before she turned to the cupboard and gathered a small soufflé bowl to hold her condiment for dipping.

"Can anybody else ride Sable? Or drive her?" Karen asked.

"Neal has never touched my vehicle in all the years we've been married, but all the Soccer Moms noticed we were uncomfortable riding in each others' minivans right before the craziness started." Francine ripped off a chunk of white meat, dipped it in her dish of mayonnaise and popped the morsel in her mouth. "I'm sorry. I'm so rude. Did you want some?"

Karen shook her head, a disgusted look on her face.

Francine's stomach growled even louder though she gnawed on the chicken breasts. If it weren't for the hunger gnawing on her stomach, she could have fallen asleep on her feet after everything that had happened since Penny woke her up this morning. She'd probably need an extra box or two of Long Johns for her breakfast at the rate things were going. And that was assuming The Bake Shoppe would be open tomorrow morning.

"Do the other ladies' powers affect them the way yours does to you?" Karen asked. "You've barely stopped eating in just the few hours I've known you."

Francine sighed as she tore off a bite from the thighs. How much did she really want to tell Karen? She seemed all right. The hunter wasn't possessed or anything. She was saved from answering by Karen's phone ringing.

Karen grimaced as she glanced at the caller ID. "Hey, Father McAvoy! What's up?"

"Do you realize your pictures are all over the news broadcasts?" The priest's tone was mild compared to his words.

More surprising was that the hunter had put her phone on speaker.

She winced, but she firmly said, "Those idiots at the graveyard planned to shoot the rising dead, Father. I followed Francine's lead because she's a Horseman, ur, Soccer Mom of the Apocalypse. If she's one of God's chosen, then she outranks me."

"This isn't a matter of who's in charge," Father McAvoy said. "It's a matter of staying in the shadows so we don't alarm the public."

"Father, with all due respect, the dead rising from their graves is already alarming the public," Karen said. "That's why those people were at the cemetery with guns, and they wanted to take potshots at a bunch of confused undead."

"Are you coming back to the rectory, tonight?"

"No, I'm going to stay at Francine's." Karen glanced at Francine. "She said it was okay, and she has Penny's recently risen mother-in-law here along with a little girl named Rose who was climbing out of her own grave when Francine and I ran into each other."

"Actually, I feel better if you and Laura are both there to watch Francine's back," he said. "Reporters and frightened people are both dangerous in their own way. Mix them together and—" He paused. "H-how is Laura doing with all this?"

"I'm doing just fine, Deke." Laura and Rose had entered the kitchen so quietly Francine hadn't heard them. Rose was now dressed in a bright pink unicorn t-shirt and a floaty gauze princess skirt Brittany had worn for a dance recital and Halloween.

The priest's voice gentled. "It's been a long time."

"Yes, it has." The corners of Laura's mouth twitched. "Longer than I realized when I first woke up this morning."

"Well—" Father McAvoy cleared his throat. "If there's anything I can do to help you—"

"Check with Father Perez," Francine said around a mouthful of leg. "Dani was supposed to call him." She swallowed her chicken before she explained about the Red Cross set-up at the high school and their need for supplies.

The priest chuckled. "It sounds like you have things well in hand, Francine. I'll leave you ladies to your evening."

"I'll text you with any status changes, Father." Karen ended the call.

The odor of fear wafted from Rose despite her recent bath.

"Sweetie, what's wrong?" Francine asked.

"Wh-what is that thing?" A shaking forefinger pointed at Karen. No, not Karen. Her phone.

Francine pulled some obscure facts out of her brain based on when Rose was alive. "Have you ever heard of Samuel Morse?"

The girl nodded solemnly. "I read a story about him in the newspaper. Papa says Mister Morse is mad, and no device could ever deliver a message faster than a man with a good horse."

Francine grabbed a paper towel and wiped chicken grease from her fingers. There was no longer any way to avoid telling Rose the truth. "Sweetie, why don't you have a seat at the table? Would you like a glass of milk or maybe some juice?"

"Milk, please." The girl walked with a sedated glide across the kitchen floor, and she smoothed her skirt before she sat on one of the kitchen chairs.

Her manners were so different than Brittany's mix of sports and glitter behavior. Rose reminded Francine of her grandmother who always insisted that her granddaughters act like ladies. Guilt tugged at Francine's heart. There had been far too many times when she'd given the same lecture to Brittany. It was a wonder her daughter didn't resent her.

Francine retrieved a glass from the cupboard, poured the milk, and delivered it to Rose. "Here you go."

"Thank you."

Francine sat next to the little girl. "The box Karen was using to talk to a co-worker is a more advanced version of Mister Morse's device. She can use it to talk to people or write notes to them." She pulled her own phone out of her tote and set it on the table. "They are quite common in our time."

"Wh-what do you mean by your time?" Rose's bottom lip trembled.

"Rose, what year is it?"

"It's 1848," she whispered. "Isn't it?"

"No, sweetie." Francine wished she could spare the girl, but Rose could get hurt by not understanding the modern world. "It's two hundred years later."

"I-I should be dead." Rose trembled. "M-my mama and papa . . ."

"Are buried in the Oakfield Cemetery." Francine didn't want to say the next part. "Like you were."

"B-but I'm alive." Rose protested.

"You're like me." Laura pulled a chair closer to the girl and sat. "I rose out of my grave early this morning. Francine and I found you as you were climbing out of yours."

"I was dead?" Rose's eyes glistened.

"We both were," Laura stated.

Francine's heart threatened to break. No one should have to go through this confusion and agony. How could God do this to someone? No wonder Penny questioned her faith when Justine had leukemia. All this madness made Francine question the Almighty herself.

"How long were you dead?" Rose whispered.

"Only two years." Laura's smile was tremulous at best. "In some ways, it's harder for me. Returning from the dead scared my husband and sons."

"Is this—is this the Rapture?" Rose asked.

"No," Francine said sternly.

"But you said you were Famine." Rose frowned.

"Technically speaking, no I didn't." Francine smirked at the memory of Hank and his friends. "The idiots with the guns said I was."

"But you didn't deny it." Rose shot her an accusatory look that only an eight-year-old girl could master.

"Okay, you're right." Francine fixed the child with a stern expression. "I may be one of the Four Horsemen, but we are doing everything we can to stop the Apocalypse."

"What if you can't?" Rose whispered.

"I can't ask you to trust us," Francine said. "We need to earn your trust by actually stopping it."

And by accidentally outing the Soccer Moms, she may have just made stopping the Apocalypse next to impossible.

Chapter 18

Francine was a little surprised how well Rose took the news of her death. There were a few tears and some questions about why her parents hadn't risen from their graves, none of which Francine could answer. She still had a copy of the history paper Brittany had written on her laptop. Rose was reading it out loud to Laura and Karen when Neal entered the kitchen, his arms loaded with plastic bags.

"I hope we have enough food in the house for the next couple days," he grumbled. "You aren't getting anywhere around town without being followed by reporters."

Francine winced. "Did they give you a hard time?"

"All the way to The Steak House." He set the food bags on the table. "I know Officer Pence has been giving Penny a rough time lately, but he had no problem ticketing everybody for being out after curfew."

Francine paused in pulling out drinking glasses from the cupboard for the adults and looked at her husband. "You got a ticket?"

"Ironically, not me." Neal grinned. "Dan Park was in charge of the checkpoint at the interstate exit. He cut me some slack because I'd be home before the curfew went into effect if I left right at that moment. However, the pack following me all got ticketed."

"But if the police hold them until curfew, they can challenge the tickets," Karen said.

"Which is why many of them have reckless driving and public nuisance charges filed against them as well." Neal grinned.

"I'm not sure that was the best way to handle things." Francine bit her bottom lip.

Neal joined her by the cupboard. "Honey, according to Dan, you made an impression on the police who responded to the cemetery. Not only did you keep your head in a dangerous situation, you offered to help the people coming back from the dead. He said the mayor and city council aren't sure what to do next. The high school gym is filling up fast."

"What about the churches?" Laura asked. "Surely, the girls can pull in their resources. They're making calls as we speak."

"We need to take this one step at a time—" The unmistakable sense of demons nearby interrupted Francine. Outside. The back deck.

"Sable! The backyard!"

Her horse whinnied in answer.

She turned to Karen. "Demons. Keep everybody away from the windows."

"Downstairs," Neal added.

While Karen herded Neal and their undead guests down the stairs, Francine strode for the French doors, her scales in her hand. She stepped out onto the deck.

For once, there was no wind. No hum of vehicles. No barking.

Nothing.

Light from the kitchen filtered past the sheer curtains on the French doors and highlighted the figures standing on the other side of the covered swimming pool. But underneath the four shadowed forms, she could see the twisted visages of the demons who possessed the humans. With a soft huff behind her, Sable indicated her presence.

"Leave." Francine wished her voice exhibited more command, not come out in a breathy whisper. She sounded like a starlet trying to seduce a president.

Or a dying woman.

"Or what?" one of the demons mocked. "How will you explain the dead in your domain if you kill these bodies?"

It had a point. While her sisters possessed lovely sharp, pointy implements that could kill the demons without hurting the human host, all she had were her scales. The best she could do was whack the crap out of the humans the demons wore. She needed a good bluff.

No, she needed a great bluff. It had been a long time since she was banned from every casino in Las Vegas.

"Do you truly wish to die for a prince who despises you?" She swung her scales with each step she took across the redwood deck. "If he wins the coming battle, do you really believe he will allow you in Heaven? He's not one of you. He may be the ruler of Hell, but underneath everything, he's still an archangel."

"You are the enemy," the first demon spat. "You have been killing our kind from the beginning."

"The beginning of what?" she mocked in return. "This month? When you kidnapped my sister's child and tried to kill us?" When she got a good look at the first demon, her heart leapt into her throat. Jermaine Richards. Their next door neighbor. Next to him was his wife Sherlyn and their teen sons, Korbin and Kirby.

The Richards had spare keys to the Astins' house. They watched each others' homes when they were away on vacations or visits with the grandparents in Florida.

And the odds were these four were a diversion. Why did they need a diversion? She had two Vatican demon hunters guarding Neal and Rose.

The demon wearing Sherlyn smiled an ugly, leering smile. "It will not be as easy to harm these humans we wear. Your precious morals will not allow it."

Francine flipped her scales so she held them like a baseball bat. "Considering I used these to whack the demon possessing the husband of Pestilence, I don't think I'll have a problem beating you senseless."

"Instead of threatening each other, let us discuss a trade." The demon wearing Kirby stepped forward. "Give us the dead, and we will leave you and your two mortals in peace."

"They're not dead anymore," Francine snapped.

"They are unnatural, even by our standards," the demon inside Korbin said. "They need to be returned to the earth. We will dispose of them for you."

"They are God's faithful," she shot back. "I would never give them to you."

Behind her, the French doors opened.

"Get back inside—" Francine started to turn when someone, or something, grabbed her by the back of her tattered robes and tossed her through the open doors and across her kitchen.

She crashed headfirst into her brand-new, sub-zero, stainless-steel refrigerator with a resounding *BONG!*

A woman cursed nearby as someone or something yanked Francine upright. Mr. Treeger from across the street, or rather the demon possessing him, wrapped his fingers around her throat and slammed her head into the refrigerator again.

Water exploded around them. The godawful odor of burnt hair filled the air. Mr. Treeger's howl abruptly cut off as black smoke spilled from his mouth, nose, and ears. Francine landed on her ass as her poor neighbor's puppeteer clipped his strings. Mr. Treeger landed on top of her.

If it weren't for Famine's powers and stamina, she'd have more than one broken bone.

The smoke searched for a new victim. It headed straight for Karen.

Karen? Why wasn't she in the friggin' basement?

"*Te custodem et patronum sancta veneratur Ecclesia; te gloriatur defensore adversus terrestrium et infernorum nefarias potestates*—" the demon hunter recited. White light flashed within the black cloud, just like it had at Alcott's Restaurant when Penny's father-in-law and Father Perez had exorcised the demon inhabiting Oakfield attorney Gwen Taylor. But the demon surged toward Karen.

If they survived this encounter, Francine would petition the Vatican for a shorter exorcism ritual. The current one took too long.

She rolled to her feet and swung her scales through the smoky demon wailing over the kitchen table. The smoke exploded into ash.

Well, that was an interesting development. She could kill demons if they weren't inside a human.

Out on the deck, Sable neighed, and her hooves stamped on the deck.

Francine stuck her emaciated index finger and thumb into her mouth and blew a shrill whistle. "In here, girl!"

Sable whirled and entered the kitchen. After the Soccer Moms' ride through the city to rescue Justine, Francine had consulted with her sorority big sister by e-mail, claiming she was writing a science fiction story. Gretchen worked at CERN as a quantum physicist. As near as she could explain, Sable and the other horses slipped into a side dimension to get around obstacles in what humans perceived as reality. However, Francine suspected when Sable was a minivan she could be physically injured.

Just like the four demons outside still had to use the French doors because they possessed humans.

The doors the demon in Mr. Treeger had conveniently left open when it tossed Francine inside the kitchen.

Chapter 19

Cold wind and the demons inside the Richards family charged into Francine's kitchen.

"Kill the hunter," the demon possessing Jermaine growled. "I'll take care of the Horseman." It strode across the kitchen area.

"That's Soccer Mom to you," Francine shot back. She shouldered her scales like a baseball bat.

"Heads up!" Karen launched a very full water balloon at the demon's back. She must have found Brittany's stash in the basement.

The demon dove out of the way. Francine didn't have time to duck. The water balloon hit her square in the chest and exploded.

Before she could blink the water out of her eyes, something heavy smashed into her head. Wood cracked. If she were normal right now, her skull would have caved in. She rolled to her right, swiping the holy water from her eyes as she moved.

The demon wearing Jermaine held half of her antique maple table Great-aunt Ruth had given to her and Neal for their wedding. The demon raised the table to slam the jagged edge into her.

She grabbed Jermaine's leg and shifted her vision. Jermaine was in there, his garnet soul chipped at the edges and surrounded by a cloud of soot. Sherlyn was sick. Cancer. He wasn't sure he could go on without her. And they had confessed about her medical condition to the boys last night.

Crap. No wonder the Richards were easy pickings for the demons.

Francine reached inside for the demon soot and scraped it out of

Jermaine. Her vision shifted back to reality as an unconscious Jermaine landed on top of her. Demon smoke swirled next to the ceiling, but Karen wasn't reciting the exorcism prayer.

Climbing to her feet, Francine found out why. The demon in Sherlyn held the hunter bent backwards over the breakfast bar, choking her. Karen grabbed the closest thing at hand, which unfortunately was the jack o'lantern cookie jar Grandma Coy had made for Francine. The demon hunter whacked the ceramic over Sherlyn's head. The jar shattered, but it didn't stop the demon inside Sherlyn from throttling Karen.

Sable kept the other two demons back. However, the horse stomped on appliances and cracked ceramic floor tiles left and right in order to prevent the demons from piling on Karen.

Francine snatched her scales from the floor and threw them through the demon hovering near the ceiling. Once again, a bright flash of light filled the kitchen. The scales landed with a metallic clatter in the sink. Ash fell in soft flakes over the broken flooring. She leapt over the breakfast bar and jerked the second demon off Karen.

Sherlyn's soul was a soft golden topaz, and unlike Jermaine's, it had a large crack through the middle. Francine repeated the same scraping maneuver to clear the demon out of Sherlyn's body. Her neighbor turned into a deadweight in her arms.

"Karen?" Francine carefully settled Sherlyn in the floor.

"Still here," the demon hunter wheezed.

"I need the exorcism prayer to hold that—" Francine jabbed her index finger at the demon swirling around the kitchen ceiling. "—while I deal with the other two." She reached over, grabbed a water balloon, and smashed it on top of Karen's head.

"Hey!" the demon hunter protested as she swiped dripping blue locks out of her eyes.

"I can't have them possessing you while my back is turned."

"*Sancte Míchael Archángele, defénde nos in próelio*—" Karen began.

"Sable, back!"

Her horse snorted and danced back into the breakfast nook, kicking aside the other half of the table and splintering a couple of chairs in the process.

The demons rushed her, and she grabbed them by the throat. The boys' souls were orange tourmaline. Korbin's shaded more toward a reddish orange, and Kirby's was a yellowish orange. Francine carefully scraped off the demons surrounding their souls and gently lowered the boys to the broken floor tiles.

Overhead, the three incorporeal demons spun like a mini tornado with strikes of lightning while Karen continued reciting her exorcism prayer. Francine retrieved her scales from the sink and threw them through the smoky vortex.

A heavy *thunk* rattled all the cupboards. This flash of white light was even more brilliant. Francine shaded her eyes. Her scales crashed to the floor, probably breaking even more tiles.

When she could see again, the demons were gone. However, a huge chunk of plaster was missing in the center of the kitchen ceiling. Two skull-sized dents marred the finish of the sub-zero refrigerator. The toaster oven and the Cuisinart were nothing more than broken bits. And it was easier to count the intact ceramic floor tiles than the cracked and broken ones.

At least, none of the Richards were physically injured. She crossed to Mr. Treeger and gently turned him over to inspect his injuries. Most of the silver hair on the back of his head had been singed off, and first-degree burns marred his scalp and neck. Otherwise, he seemed to be all right.

Francine looked up at Karen. "We need to work on your aim with water balloons."

Chapter 20

Francine stood, but a wave of dizziness forced her to grab the refrigerator handle to stay upright. She was suddenly exhausted and starving. Thankfully, one of the bar stools were still intact. She staggered over to it and sagged on the seat.

Karen looked around the destroyed kitchen. "It may take me a while to pay you back for the damage."

Francine giggled. Which turned into a belly chuckle. Soon she was laughing so hard, she unceremoniously slipped from the stool and plopped on the floor amid the debris, tears running down her cheeks. Karen circled the bar, eying Francine uncertainly.

When her mirth died, she looked up at the demon hunter. "It kind of serves me right for what I did to Penny's house."

"What did you do to her place?"

"Knocked a demon right through her front door." Francine grinned. "While it was closed." She looked around her. "I need to text her some pictures. She's going to love this."

Her stomach rumbled, a reminder she hadn't eaten since her chicken and mayo snack. She pushed herself to her feet. The bags of take-out were gone. "Wait a minute. What happened to the take-out Neal brought home?"

Karen chuckled. "It's downstairs. Laura swore she wasn't fighting demons on an empty stomach."

"Guess it has been a while since we had lunch." Francine crossed over to the basement door and shoved aside the half of the kitchen table leaning against it. She opened the door and called out, "Everyone okay down there?"

Laura appeared at the foot of the steps, Karen's gun in her hands and aimed up the stairwell. "Prove you're Francine."

She sighed. If she let Famine loose again, she'd eat everything in the house in one sitting. Or worse, affect her family with her hunger. She settled on reciting the Lord's Prayer.

On the third line, Laura said, "That's enough." She lowered the weapon. "You coming down to eat?"

"Uh, I think I need to take my neighbors home now that they are no longer possessed," Francine responded.

Neal appeared next to Laura. "Which neighbors?"

"The Richards and Mr. Treeger." Francine glanced behind her. "And Mr. Treeger's injured from a holy water balloon."

Neal pursed his lips. "Eat my steak and the two I got for you first before you take them home." He disappeared from view.

"Should we go back upstairs?" Rose's high-pitched voice sounded curious, not scared, which relieved Francine to no end.

"You and Laura go ahead and finish your dinners down here. We'll let you know when the mess in the kitchen is cleaned up," Neal answered. "I don't want you to cut your feet on the broken things."

"Sable, garage," Francine murmured.

The steed snorted an obvious negation.

"Yes," Francine hissed. "You know he freaks when you're in the house."

Sable stomped back to the garage via the side dimension, making sure Francine knew of her displeasure.

Neal reappeared, carrying two of The Steak House bags.

When he reached the first floor, he looked around the kitchen and shook his head. "I guess this is payback after what you did to the Hudsons' house."

"Except I did both." Francine couldn't help herself. She started laughing like a maniac again.

"Sit down and eat, honey." Neal placed his hand on the small of her back and gently guided her toward the remaining bar stool.

"But I can't—"

"I ordered you two full meals. Eat your steaks. I'll keep the rest warm." Neal set the bags on the breakfast bar. "While you and Karen take everyone home, I'll broil some cheeseburgers—" He turned toward the refrigerator and remained silent for several seconds.

"Neal?" Suddenly, none of this was as funny as it had been a moment ago.

"I'm not trying to be mean, but please tell me those dents in the refrigerator are from your skull." He looked at her. "Otherwise, we're going to have a problem explaining why you slammed our neighbors' heads into our fridge door."

♦   💀   ♦

Francine tucked each of the Richards in their beds while Karen drew protective symbols with a transparent medium over all the upstairs windows and doors.

"Can I help?" Francine followed Karen down to the first floor.

"It's better if you start with visible latex or acrylic so you can see what you're doing."

"Why does the transparent stuff work if no one can see it?"

Karen grinned as she painted designs by the Richards' front door. "They're visible under black light." She finished and set the bottle and brush on a paper towel she'd grabbed from the kitchen before she pulled a mini flashlight from her bag.

She flipped off the living room lights before she shone the vaguely purple flashlight on the wall where she'd drawn symbols. Under the ultraviolet rays, the symbols shown as bright as day.

"What happens if the people you're trying to protect paint the living room because they don't know the symbols are there?"

"That's the beauty of paint." Karen picked up her accoutrements and headed for the dining room. "The runes are still there. In fact, the layers of additional paint preserves the protection symbols. As long as the black light paint isn't damaged or removed somehow, they will protect this place as long as it's a home." She began drawing the same figures on the dining room's hand-painted floral pattern. "Which means you need to be more careful about throwing demons through walls."

Francine sighed. "I've never been in a fight in my life until this week. I didn't think I was capable of the kind of violence I've done."

"The reason you're fighting makes a huge difference." Karen moved clockwise to the next window. "In your case, you're not trying to take something from someone. You're trying to save the world."

When they were finished in the Richards' home, Francine carried a still unconscious Mr. Treeger back to his house. His gas stove prompted an excuse for his injuries, and she relayed her idea to the demon hunter who agreed. While Karen drew protective symbols over his windows and doors, Francine settled him stomach-down on his couch, placing pillows under his chest and head before she ran back to her house for her bottle of aloe vera gel.

On her way back through Mr. Treeger's kitchen, she set his cast iron skillet on the counter next to the stove. She didn't like lying to him, but she'd already done more than enough damage by exposing herself as Famine. Thank goodness, her family had visited with Mr. Treeger several times. She grabbed a clean dish towel from the drawer.

Francine perched on the edge of the couch and carefully brushed away the singed silver hair on the back of Mr. Treeger's head. She didn't need to look at his soul to know what troubled him. His precious German Shepard Heidi had passed away at the beginning of spring. Mr. Treeger hadn't recovered. He'd broken into tears when Brittany had suggested he get another dog at their Fourth of July party.

The demons' actions made Francine grit her teeth as she stroked the cooling gel over her neighbor's scalp. They hit people at their lowest. When they needed the most help.

And if she didn't get her own anger under control, she'd scare the hell out of Mr. Treeger.

She slathered more gel on the first degree burns on his neck and upper back when he groaned and stirred. One eye opened and he peered up at her. "Ms. Coy-Astin, I don't think your husband would be happy about you rubbing my back."

Chapter 21

"I'm putting aloe on your burns." Francine wiped her hands on the towel. "Does your head hurt any place in particular?"

"Just the back." His fingers probed his singed scalp. "But it feels like a burn. What happened?"

"We heard a loud bang over here. We found you and a frying pan on the floor of the kitchen." Francine stood so the older man could turn and sit upright. "You were burned and unconscious, and one of the gas burners on your stove had been turned on but wasn't lit."

Mr. Treeger frowned. "I don't remember turning on a burner."

Karen strode back into the living room. "Yeah, Francine, it was just the burner in the kitchen releasing natural gas. I didn't find any other leaks." She smiled at Mr. Treeger. "How are you feeling, sir?"

"Who the heck are you?" His frown turned to a glare.

"That's my friend, Karen." Francine gestured at the demon hunter. "She came to visit for Halloween. She was in my kitchen with me when we heard the loud noise over here."

Mr. Treeger harrumphed.

"Any bumps on your head?" Karen asked.

He reached for the back of his head again. "No, my scalp burns, my hair's missing, and I have a bit of a headache. Nothing else."

"If you were breathing methane for a bit, that would account for the headache," Francine said. "Do you want us to take you to the emergency room to make sure you don't have a concussion? You may have gotten hit in the head by the frying pan. Or are you feeling nauseous or dizzy from the natural gas?"

He glared at her. "I may be old enough to be your father, but I didn't hit myself in the head with the damn skillet. Besides, there's a damn curfew in town. How are you planning to get me to the damn hospital?"

"We can call an ambulance," Karen suggested.

"I don't need an ambulance!"

"That's the problem, Mr. Treeger," Francine protested. "We're not sure exactly what happened to you. We weren't here." Maybe she was hanging around demons too much. She was using a bit of the truth to coat her lies.

"How about a compromise?" Karen suggested. "Francine calls you every hour for the rest of the night. If you don't answer your phone, we call 9-1-1."

He sighed. "Fine. Let's do that." He looked at Francine. "But if I'm cranky in the morning, I'm blaming you."

She smiled. "I totally understand, Mr. Treeger. Would you like me to bring you a coffee from Java's Palace after I run my errands in the morning?"

"Cinnamon caramel macchiato," he said, but there was a bit of twinkle back in his eyes. "Large and tell Penny extra hot."

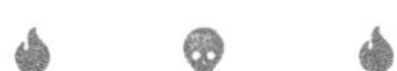

Francine and Karen returned to the Astin house to find Rose helping Laura sweep up and bag the broken items while Neal cooked hamburgers on the stovetop grill. The little girl had donned Brittany's flip-flops so she wouldn't cut her feet on the debris. All of Brittany's other shoes had been far too large for the eight-year-old.

"Well?" he asked.

"I need to check on all the neighbors tomorrow." Francine shook her head. "It's one thing to come after us Soccer Moms. It's another to come after the people we care about."

He made a derisive noise. "Those bastards already proved they'd stop at nothing when they kidnapped Justine—"

Francine held up her hands to stop him, but it was too late. Laura pivoted, an appalled expression etched on her face.

"What's this about demons taking my granddaughter?"

"We got her back safely," Francine said. "She's fine."

"Penny's not that foolish," Laura bit out. "How did they get Justine?"

Francine grimaced. She couldn't half-ass her way through a lie like she had with Mr. Treeger. "Gene got possessed. That's how the demons were able to grab Justine."

"Gene?" Laura blinked. "No. How?" Karen caught the broom handle that slipped from Laura's grasp.

"Can we talk about this later?" Francine inclined her head at Rose.

The girl lifted her chin. "I'm not a baby. Of course, there are demons. You said it is the end of the world."

"That's what we're trying to stop," Francine said.

"Let's finish eating," Neal changed the subject. "Have you ever had ice cream, Rose?"

"I've had snow ice cream," she said. "We make it at the first snowfall of the year." Her lower lip trembled. "Or we used to."

Maybe Rose wasn't handling the situation as well as Francine assumed.

"Now, we can have ice cream all year long," Neal said in his best salesman voice. "What sounds good? We've got mint chocolate chip, cookie dough, rocky road—"

"You put rocks in your ice cream?" Rose shot him a suspicious look.

Neal laughed. "No real rocks, I promise. It's chocolate ice cream with marshmallow fluff and almonds."

"Chocolate?" Glee lit up the little girl's face. "Santa brought me chocolate one year for Christmas. It's better than penny candy!"

"Rocky road it is then." Neal flipped the burgers onto a serving platter and turned off the grill before he strode over to the fridge. He pulled out the pint of rocky road. "What's your flavor, Laura?"

"Cookie dough, please." Penny's mother-in-law didn't look one bit happy, but she understood the need to focus on Rose, and not her own upset over Justine's abduction by a possessed Gene.

There were enough unbroken chairs and stools they could gather around the breakfast bar. Neal dished out ice cream for Rose and Laura.

Only after her fourth hamburger and all her side dishes from the meals Neal brought home did the ache in Francine's stomach subside. She and Neal split the pint of mint chocolate chip ice cream. Karen dug into the remaining cookie dough while she and Francine told the rest what had happened with Mr. Treeger.

"How about I stay up and check on him?" Neal said.

"But you need to be at work tomorrow morning," Francine protested.

"Already called my managers, and they are passing the word that we will be closed for the weekend." He shrugged. "I'm giving everyone paid time off. There's nothing in the employee manual that covers relatives coming back from the dead, and I can't see anyone shopping for cars for the next couple of days."

"Will the demons come back here?" Rose eyed each of the adults as if daring them to lie to her or avoid the subject again.

"The ones that were here tonight won't be coming back," Francine assured the girl. "Karen and I killed them."

"But there's more, isn't there?"

"Yes, but Karen knows how to keep them out so they can't get back into our house." Francine looked at the demon hunter. "And I didn't say thank you for helping me with our neighbors. Thanks. I really appreciate your assistance. Could you show me how to draw those sigils?"

Karen nodded. "Let me take care of your place first."

"I could use the practice, too," Laura said. "You got some extra paint?"

"It's UV-reactive clear," Karen said hesitantly.

"Honey, I grew up in the Sixties and Seventies." Laura chuckled. "I was doing psychedelic stuff before your parents were born." She turned to Francine. "And when we're done, you and I are going to have a talk, young lady."

"After I warn the rest of the Soccer Moms." Francine's conversation with her friends would be bad enough. The last thing Francine needed was a lecture about safety from someone who didn't know the first thing about what it was like being a Soccer Mom.

Chapter 22

Francine tucked Rose into Brittany's bed and read her a couple of stories while Laura and Karen painted the invisible sigils throughout the house. It didn't take long for Rose to fall asleep despite being mesmerized by Brittany's bubbly nightlight.

Coming back from the dead was an awful lot for an eight-year-old to handle. Coming back two centuries after her death—well, there was a reason Jebediah Hauser ran around Main Street like a maniac this morning.

Francine retreated to her bedroom, linked the Soccer Moms on a conference call, and told them about the demon attack in her kitchen. Penny, Wila, and Dani didn't find the damage to the Astins' kitchen as funny as Francine.

"You took on a whole nest by yourself?" Wila shouted. "Are you insane?"

"I wasn't by myself," Francine shot back. "I had two demon hunters backing me up. Plus I figured out how to remove a possessing demon without using holy water." She explained how she cleaned the demon off a human soul. "Then I whack the smoke with my scales. Dead demon."

Wila burst out laughing. "So you flush the game out and kill it?"

"That isn't funny," Dani chided.

"If you don't see demons as a pest, an infection or a parasite, how do you view them?" Penny asked.

"They can talk. They have intelligence. Maybe they don't know any better because they don't have souls," Dani said crossly.

"I think we know some demon hunters who would disagree with you," Francine said. "Does Edward know how to draw protection sigils to guard a home from a demon invasion?"

"The paint he ordered arrived today," Penny said. "Apparently, he special-ordered it after our altercation with Seth Rimmon last Saturday. It's a clear UV-reactive paint so the symbols aren't obvious to civilians without a black light."

"And I had a couple of extra cans of white spray paint after refurbishing my bedroom suit over the summer," Wila said. "He talked me through drawing the sigils over the phone." She sighed. "I'm glad I have extra paint for each room to cover up these weird-ass symbols tomorrow before Derek gets home."

Francine's face heated. After Karen's attitude about teaching her the sigils, she was a little ticked Edward trusted Wila enough to do her protection symbols without supervision.

"Watch your backs if you're not at home, and definitely look out for the newly risen," Francine said. "For some reason, the nest that attacked me wanted Laura and Rose."

"Did they say why?" Wila asked.

"We didn't get to that part of the conversation," Francine said dryly. "They were too busy using my skull to dent my refrigerator."

Thankfully, Penny changed the subject and relayed the gossip of whose dead relatives had shown up at the homes of various members of the Oakfield Parents Association. The Youth League's soccer games for tomorrow had been postponed despite OPA President Courtney Lasser raising a fuss. Oakfield's mayor overruled her, given the declared state of emergency for the county. And every member of the OPA and the churches the other Soccer Moms had contacted volunteered supplies for the risen dead sheltering at the high school gymnasium.

"I did talk to Pastor Burns on your behalf," Penny said. "We need to meet him at First Methodist in the morning for the supplies. He said the

Ladies' Auxiliary already have cots set up for the risen parishioners who showed up there today, and they have room for more if the city needs it."

"Just be careful, ladies," Francine said. "I had a heck of a time taking out five demons when one of the demon hunters was throwing balloons filled with holy water in my face."

Her friends cracked up.

"I'm glad I have a use for the water balloons I confiscated from my son," Dani said between giggles.

"Can you pick up some extra holy water for us from Father Perez tomorrow when you swing by Saint Michael's?" Wila suggested. "It sounds like we're going to need it."

"I will," Dani said.

"I'll see you guys in the morning." Francine ended the call and flopped on her back. Had it only been this morning when Penny called her in a total panic over her dead mother-in-law on her doorstep? It felt like it was months ago. If her life kept up this pace, she'd give herself a stress-related heart attack.

Or starve to death because of her alter ego's powers.

When Francine entered the kitchen, the other three adults waited for her. Thank goodness, Neal had poured her a glass of white zinfandel. The wine might be passé now, but she preferred the light, sweet flavor. She retrieved a bag of dark chocolate raspberry truffles from the cupboard before she sat down at the breakfast bar with the others.

Neal eyed her with concern, Karen with curiosity, but Laura's expression was flat out naked hostility.

"Start from the beginning," Laura ordered.

"Well, technically, this all started when a drunk driver hit Dani's pickup as she and Mark were headed home from soccer practice—"

"That's not what I mean, and you know it, Francine Coy-Astin," Laura snapped.

"It's all wrapped up in the same thing," Francine bit back. She summarized the first couple of weeks and gave Laura a lot more detail about Penny's disastrous meeting with Seth Rimmon and his attorney.

"Frankly, Gene couldn't handle the idea of Penny being a Soccer Mom of the Apocalypse," Francine continued. "He left her Saturday night."

Laura's expression shifted from anger to horror. "But he wasn't possessed at that time, right?"

"Correct." Francine took a sip of her wine. "We think he was possessed sometime Monday evening. We think that's why Rimmon and some of his nest confronted Penny in the grocery store parking lot. They were there to keep her distracted so the rest of the nest could get to Gene."

Laura's knuckles whitened as she gripped her cup of decaffeinated green tea. "But Edward knows better."

"Gene wasn't listening to me or Edward, much less the ladies," Neal said.

Francine frowned at her husband. "When did you talk to him?"

"Monday afternoon." Neal shrugged. "For a shrink, he was being rather pig-headed about the whole situation. I couldn't talk him into staying with us or Father Perez. I didn't tell you because there was no point in stirring the pot."

She reached across the bar and grasped his hand. "Thank you for trying."

Neal squeezed her fingers. "After everything the two of them have been through, I thought their marriage was rock solid. Goes to show you don't know what goes on behind the scenes of someone's life."

Francine looked at Laura. "The demon who possessed Gene played him well enough it fooled Penny when she spoke to it on the phone later that night."

Karen made a disgusted sound low in her throat. "You mean it told her what she wanted to hear. He was stupid, he wanted to talk, let me pick up the kid from school, we'll have a family dinner, yadda, yadda, yadda."

Francine studied the demon hunter. "It's like you were there."

"Nope, they used the same playbook to kidnap me when I was younger than your kids." A shudder ran through Karen. "I was fortunate. My uncle worked for the Vatican taskforce, too, though none of us knew it at the time. He knew how to get me back and purged the demon from my dad."

She turned to Laura. "You're dang lucky Penny has friends like the other Soccer Moms. Uncle Nate had to give Mom and Aunt Coco a crash course in fighting demons. Mom lost her right eye in their battle."

"I-I'm sorry for taking my anger out on you, Francine," Laura murmured. "I should never have gone along with Ed's desire to hide our past from our boys."

"You did what you thought was best at the time," Francine said. "It's not like either of you knew Gene would marry a Soccer Mom of the Apocalypse."

"But I put my grandchildren in danger as a result of hiding the truth about our past." Laura shook her head.

"If it's any consolation, Edward's teaching our kids how to protect themselves now." Francine shot Karen a nasty look. "Including how to draw demon protection symbols on the wall. He got the paint right after he discover Seth Rimmon and his attorney were demons."

Karen cleared her throat. "Well, I guess I'd better get started teaching you, too."

Chapter 23

When Francine's alarm went off the next morning, Neal insisted he was accompanying her and the other women to the First Methodist Church, even though he'd been checking on Mr. Treeger the entire night.

Or until the normally mild Mr. Treeger made an anatomically impossible suggestion at three a.m.

But if Neal came with them, that meant they needed to bring Rose with them, too. Francine wasn't about to leave any eight-year-old home alone, even without the demons and the dead running around Oakfield.

"I can help you, Miz Francine. I helped Mama all the time with charity work," the girl said primly over breakfast.

"That settles it." Neal grinned. "We'll have extra carrying space between Sable and my sedan."

"No offence regarding any of the brands you sell, but let's take my car instead." Karen grinned. "I have more trunk space in my Charger once I clear out my gear. Assuming you don't mind I leave it here for the morning, that is."

"Are you sure you want to?" Francine asked.

"Don't worry. I'll make sure both vehicles are armed." Karen waved her bagel.

"Armed?" Rose's eyes widened. "We will all carry rifles?"

"No one's carrying a gun except the one person licensed to do so," Neal said sternly.

"Besides, the demons would have to destroy your house to get at the rest of my stuff," Karen continued. "If that happens, we have bigger problems."

Neal rolled his eyes. "Please don't give the demons any ideas."

"Let's finish our breakfast, help the people who need help, and plan not to shoot anyone." Francine glared at her husband. Laura hid her smile behind her coffee cup.

Fifteen minutes later, the five of them trooped out to the driveway. While Francine, Laura, and Rose loaded the clothes and extra personal items in the back of Sable, Neal helped Karen unload her Charger. Laura wore an envious expression, but Francine wasn't sure if it were due to the sporty sedan or that the vehicle matched the color of the demon hunter's hair. It was better not to ask.

Jermaine Richards walked over from his own yard while Karen and Neal stowed the last of her gear on the shelves in the garage. "Hey, Francine."

"Hi." From his haunted eyes, she knew what was wrong, and she couldn't say anything. Not yet anyway. She hoped he only had a few nightmares about being possessed last night. "We're headed over to our church to collect donations for the people the Red Cross are housing at the high school. Would you do me a favor and check on Mr. Treeger?"

"Sure." He hesitated a moment before he added, "Can I ask why?"

"He's got burns on the back of his head and neck. We're afraid he has a concussion, too."

"Did this happen in your kitchen?" Jermaine asked.

"No." God help her, she hated lying to anyone.

"The dead are rising from their graves, Francine." Jermaine stepped closer to her. "And you suck at lying. I remember what happened in your kitchen last night. And you looked just like you did in the video on the news . . . Famine."

Francine could feel everyone's eyes on her. She sucked in a deep breath. "Are Sherlyn and the boys physically all right?"

Jermaine nodded.

Neal stepped to her side. "What's going on with you and your family? It's bad enough to lower everyone's defenses."

"I-is that how we were possessed?" Jermaine choked out.

"Yes," Francine said.

"You know, don't you?" Pain poured from him.

"Yes."

"Know what?" Neal looked at her, then Jermaine.

"It's not my secret to tell, honey." Francine eyed Jermaine. "That's part of the problem. There's keeping things private. Then, there's keeping your fear bottled to the point you break. That's when and how they take over."

Jermaine snorted. "So, that's how they got Saul Treeger? Because of his dog?"

"Don't underestimate the power of love," she said. "Or the damage from the absence of it. Neal and I are here if you and Sherlyn want to talk. We've got to pick up donations at our church and drop them off with the Red Cross at the high school. We should be back in a couple of hours. And if The Bake Shoppe is open, I'll have Long Johns to go with our coffee."

Jermaine nodded. "I'm assuming not everyone remembers they've been possessed."

Francine shook her head. "The human mind can block a lot of trauma."

A wry smile tilted the corners of his mouth. "What's the story you told Treeger about the burns on the back of his head?"

Francine couldn't stop the chuckle that rumbled out of her. "He had a battle with his gas stove, and the stove won."

For the first time since the end of September, the stress in Jermaine's face lightened, and he laughed out loud. "I'll go check on him. Text me when you get back. And Francine?"

"Yes."

"We won't say a word about your secret identity, but you need to be careful." His serious face was back. "Those demons want the people rising from their graves, but I don't know why."

As Francine drove to the church, she kept checking her mirrors. Karen's blue Charger kept pace, but there were very few other vehicles on Oakfield's streets. Even Rose understood it was an awesome car, and she insisted Laura and she ride with Karen.

Thankfully, Neal didn't insist on driving Francine's minivan. Or maybe he understood better than she thought that Sable wouldn't let him unless it was an emergency.

"Do you mind if I ask a few questions about demon and Soccer Mom stuff?" Neal said.

"Of course not." She glanced at him, but he appeared more curious than anything.

"Clearly, Jermaine remembers what happened last night while he was possessed. Does Gene remember, too?"

"Some people do. Some don't. Some people remember bits and pieces." Francine sighed. There were worse things her husband could ask about. "The only thing Gene really remembers was his demon hit Justine, which is something Gene would never do. He's dealing with a ton of guilt that he let himself be used to harm his child.

"Penny's assistant manager Valerie remembers everything. Two of the Palace's staff, Alan and Melody, don't remember a damn thing. The rest of the baristas remember bits and pieces. Like I said to Jermaine, the human mind does some wild things to protect itself from a reality it can't handle."

"How do we prevent the demons from possessing me or Brittany?"

Francine glanced at Neal again and smiled. "Given your overall self-confidence and your love of musicals, I'm not too worried about you getting possessed."

"So, all I have to do is rap the songs from *Hamilton*?" Neal grinned.

"Penny's preference is *The Sound of Music*, but I think *Hamilton* will work just fine."

"C'mon, you'd be doing the same with *Wicked*," he teased.

Francine laughed. "I'd be singing any and all of *The Wizard of Oz*-based musicals to protect myself from a demon."

But his questions lent themselves to a worry she had been avoiding. The Soccer Moms of the Apocalypse were human. Was there anything that would stop a demon from possessing one of the sisterhood besides soaking in a bathtub full of holy water?

🔥   💀   🔥

Francine recognized several of the other vehicles when she pulled into the church parking lot. She parked next to Courtney Lasser's gold minivan. If there was a prime candidate for demon possession, it should be the president of the Oakfield Parents Association and her bitchy attitude.

Pastor Burns jogged up to Sable as Francine and Neal climbed out. With his sun-bleached hair, thin build, and black hipster glasses, he looked like many of the students at UC-Oakfield. A lot of the congregation wasn't happy with Pastor Reed's replacement, but they simply didn't like change. Not to mention Pastor Reed had been approaching eighty when he finally retired.

"You wouldn't believe the donations we've been getting! Thank you for spearheading the drive, Francine!" Yep, their new minister had that fresh out of the seminary enthusiasm.

Courtney Lasser followed him at a more leisurely pace, her arms full. "It's not like Francine has anything else to do," she sneered as she kicked at the foot control to raise the rear hatch of her vehicle. She dropped the box she carried in her minivan's cargo bay.

Reverend Burns smiled graciously at Courtney. "To each according to their gifts, Mrs. Lasser. Thank you for your contributions to the poor souls in need of succor."

Courtney sniffed and marched toward the doors to the church kitchen.

Reverend Burns turned back to Francine and lowered his voice. "I've already spoken directly with Mrs. Campbell, the head of our local Red Cross region. It's not just Oakfield seeing the dead rise though we seem to be the epicenter for the continent. Is it because of you and the other Horsemen?"

"What?" Francine tried to feign innocence.

"I do own a television." He gave her a sympathetic smile. "And I'm not stupid. If Famine exists, then so do the other Horsemen."

"Soccer Moms," Neal interjected.

"Pardon me?"

Blood heated Francine's cheeks.

"The ladies prefer to be called the Soccer Moms of the Apocalypse," Neal stated.

"Pastor, if you need to talk about this, call Father Perez at Saint Michael's," Francine murmured. "I'll text him to expect your call."

Dejection filled the young minister's face. "You spoke with another church's leader first?"

"It wasn't personal, Pastor." Neal grinned. "The poor father got dragged into the mess kicking and screaming, like the ladies did."

"How about we get our vehicles loaded?" Francine said brightly when she spotted the Lasser family approaching with more boxes. She quickly introduced the rest of her party to the pastor, everyone shook hands, and they followed the pastor to the church's kitchen doors.

"Thank you for not freaking out over the Apocalypse," Francine said once they were on the way to the high school.

Neal looked up from the text he sent to Father Perez for her. "Why wouldn't I support you, honey?"

"I didn't realize how lucky I was until I saw how Gene and Jermaine and Pastor Burns reacted to the news that the Horsemen—"

"Soccer Moms," Neal interjected.

"Soccer Moms were real," she finished.

"You've got to cut Gene and Jermaine a little slack after getting possessed." Neal patted her thigh. "And Pastor Burns was a little envious you didn't come to him first because of all the crap he's gotten from the older members of the congregation. Let's face it. Pastor Reed baptized my parents."

"So why didn't you freak out when I showed you?"

"Honestly?"

She looked at him. His face was beet red, and he stared at the phone in his hand. "Honestly," she whispered.

"I'm embarrassed to say I got a cheap thrill that you had less hair as Famine than I did."

"Oh, honey." She ached for him. "I told you before I love you for you, not for the follicles on your scalp."

"Funny thing is that's why I'm not worried about getting possessed." He chuckled as he patted his toupee. "I've got everything a man could want except a full head of hair. And I know damn well no demon could deliver on that deal without turning my life into something from *The Twilight Zone*."

"If it's any consolation, I fear I'll look like Famine permanently some day."

"Only when we have side-by-side beds in the nursing home." He squeezed her thigh.

"You don't want Brittany to take care of us in our old age?"

"I'm sorry, honey, but I don't want to die on Hello Kitty bed sheets."

Francine burst out laughing. It was the first time she had an honest belly laugh in the last three weeks, and it felt pretty damn good.

Chapter 24

The teachers' parking lot was packed with vehicles when Francine guided Sable into the high school's drive, including patrol cars and other emergency vehicles. The police maintained a single lane lined with orange traffic cones up to the gym's outside doors, then out to the street again. They'd halt three vehicles in front of the gym, and volunteers unloaded while the drivers stayed inside their cars, vans, and trucks. Francine had to give the OPD and the Red Cross kudos for the efficiency of their operation.

When it was her turn for unloading, Officer Graham stepped up to the driver's window and motioned for her to roll it down. She jabbed the buttons for the back hatch and the window.

"Hi, Officer Graham!" She smiled. "What can I do for you?"

"Mayor Oldham wants to speak with you." He pointed at a couple of empty spots marked with temporary signs saying, "Reserved". "Park there, and then I'll escort you inside."

What the heck would the mayor want with her? The tingle of Famine's power rose within her. Francine hoped this wouldn't take long. She didn't have much breakfast this morning because she thought picking up and dropping off the supplies for the risen dead would be a quick trip.

"We've got friends in the Charger behind us." She jabbed a thumb toward the rear of her minivan. "They're staying at our house. Can they pull into one of the reserved spots long enough for Neal to give them our house keys?"

"No problem." Officer Graham walked down to Karen's car and spoke with her.

"Why would the mayor want to speak with you?" Neal murmured.

The woman in the Red Cross vest at the back of Sable yelled, "All clear. Thank you."

"With my luck, it's about the video on last night's news." Francine tapped the button to close the hatch, shifted gears, and guided Sable toward the reserved spots Officer Graham had pointed out to her while Neal fished his house keys out of his jeans pocket. "They didn't have a chance to program the biometric scanner for their guests yet. You should go home with Karen."

"Not gonna happen, babe." He rolled down his window as Karen stepped out of her car.

"I don't like the idea of leaving you two alone here," the demon hunter muttered as she accepted the keys from him.

Sable vibrated beneath Francine's left buttock, and she looked in the direction her minivan/horse indicated. A white minivan the same make and model as Sable was parked in the next aisle, six spots down.

"Is that Silver?"

Sable hummed via the heater fan.

Francine turned back to Karen. "Penny's already here. Take Laura and Rose home. If the fertilizer is about to hit the spinning turbine, I don't want them anywhere near me and Penny. If you don't hear from me or Neal in two hours, call Father McAvoy and ask him what your next step should be."

"We need you and your sisters if we want any hope to stop the end of the world." Karen narrowed her eyes. "I may not be able to get you out of jail or the hospital if the local authorities lock you up because they think you are batshit crazy. You got lucky talking down those people with the guns at the cemetery last night."

"And you're the only one I've got who knows how to protect Rose and isn't eligible for Medicare," Francine said. "Please don't make me beg, Karen."

"Because she will," Neal quipped. "It isn't pretty."

"Fine," the demon hunter said between gritted teeth, but her expression said there would be hell to pay if Francine ended up in jail or the psych ward. Karen climbed back into her car and drove out of the parking lot. Thank goodness, she stuck with her assumption Francine outranked her among the servants of the Lord.

Francine wasn't sure what she would have done if the demon hunter refused to protect Laura and Rose. She turned off the ignition. "Sable, listen to me. No matter what happens, you and Silver need to stay here in the parking lot."

Her seat shivered.

"I promise Penny and I will call you two if, and that's if, we actually need you." She patted the dashboard. "My guess is this will be normal human trouble, not demon trouble, this time."

A fan belt whined.

"Be a good girl."

A puff of steam seeped from the hood in grudging acquiescence.

Francine and Neal climbed out of their vehicle. Francine pressed the fob to lock the minivan. The lights flashed normally, but the horn sounded like someone blowing a raspberry.

He snickered. "I don't know why you bother. I doubt anyone could steal her."

"Force of habit," she responded, though her husband had a point. On the other hand, she didn't want Sable to pound a potential thief into pulp for climbing into the minivan and trying to hotwire her.

Officer Graham waited for her and Neal at the beginning of the line of vehicles delivering supplies. He waved for them to follow him and escorted them into the gym.

Inside, Francine's heart lodged in her throat. The high school gym didn't look like an aid center after a tornado or flood. It resembled a refugee camp in a wore-torn country. Complete with dirty injured people, vacant expressions of shock, weeping, and armed guards. If she had any doubts about taking in Rose last night, they were destroyed by the packed cots in the high school.

She glanced at Neal. He wore the same somber expression she was sure she did as he looked at the recently risen dead.

"I'm glad you brought Rose home with you," he whispered. "She's too delicate for this."

"No, she's tough like Brittany." Francine clasped his hand in hers and squeezed it. "But I still wouldn't want our daughter to be alone in an alien world."

Officer Graham continued through the doors on the opposite side of the gym, past the atrium/study hall, and toward the administration offices near the front of the huge building. He knocked on the door to the principal's office before he partially opened it and stuck his head through the gap.

"The Astins are here."

"Bring them in, Rick," a female voice said.

The policeman opened the door wider and waved for Francine and Neal to enter. Mayor Oldham leaned against the front of the principal's desk. She was roughly ten years older than Francine. The mayor's silver-threaded dark hair was pulled into a ponytail, like most other moms in Oakfield. But she had the feral air of a street-smart cat. Oakfield may be a suburb, but it had the ruthlessness in politics as Chicago itself.

Police Chief Wright stood to the right of Mayor Oldham, his arms crossed, the quintessential tough guy pose. However, Wright had the physique even at fifty to back it up. He'd won the Chicago Triathlon four years straight in his twenties. He did his best to use that minor celebrity to keep a good relationship between the police and the public in Oakfield.

Francine didn't recognize the other woman standing to the left of the mayor. The classic middle-class, middle-age helmet hairstyle made her look like a general ready for battle. Her scowl and polyester stretch pants didn't help.

Finally, a very angry Penny, with Gene at her side, stood on one side of the room and faced an equally irate Officer Miles Pence on the opposite side.

Crap. What exactly had Neal and she walked into? The tingle of Famine's power grew into a steady buzz inside Francine. She couldn't lose control. Definitely, not now.

"Thank you for talking to us, Mr. and Mrs. Astin." The mayor smiled, but the tight lines around her eyes and on her forehead indicated major tension.

"That's Ms. Coy-Astin," Francine automatically corrected.

"My apologies." Mayor Oldham inclined her head.

"What's going on?" Neal eyed Pence who glared back. "Or are stupid rumors flying around again?"

"Is it a rumor when some of the evidence was all over last night's news?" Mayor Oldham stared at Francine as if she wasn't sure whether her chain was being yanked.

"It's not that hard to fake video these days," Penny snapped. "Heck, my twelve-year-old has the computer skills to make embarrassing photos."

"Mrs. Hudson, I don't believe in supernatural bullshit despite the Jensen Ackles posters on my dorm wall in college," the mayor said dryly. "But right now, I'm a politician with dead people crawling out of their graves, not to mention walking and talking, around the city, and the good voters of Oakfield are on the edge of panicking."

She narrowed her eyes. "If Ms. Coy-Astin is Famine, then who are you, Mrs. Hudson?"

"What are you talking about?" Francine demanded. "Some jerk fakes a video, and you automatically believe we're involved in the dead rising from their graves?"

"Either Hudson was covering up for her—" Pence jabbed his index finger at Francine. "—or, more likely, Hudson is Pestilence."

Chief Wright exhaled gustily. "It would explain everyone getting sick in Java's Palace with weird diseases at the beginning of the month, Claire."

"I was thinking the same thing." The mayor smirked.

"No more free double-shot espressos for you, Chief Wright," Penny snapped.

Before Francine could say another word, Neal stepped in front of her. "What is it that you think you want from my wife, Mayor Oldham?"

"What we want is for everything to go back to normal," Pence spat.

"You're not the mayor, Miles." Neal turned to look at Francine and Penny. "Ladies, is the room clear?"

Francine frowned. She didn't like the idea of admitting what had happened with her and the rest of the Soccer Moms, but if Neal didn't think she would be hauled off in a snug white jacket, she'd go along with his ploy. But she looked at Penny to confirm her friend was okay with admitting what they were to Oakfield's top officials.

Penny dipped her head.

"None of them are possessed by demons, honey," Francine said.

"I told you," Pence crowed until her words registered in his pea brain. "Wait. What do you mean possessed by demons?"

"Is that how Seth Rimmon died?" Chief Wright glared at Francine. "You killed him because you thought he was possessed?"

"No." Francine glared back. "We haven't killed any humans."

"But that means you have killed?" the mayor prodded.

"We can kill possessing demons without us harming the human host," Penny said. "But that doesn't mean the demons don't do a ton of mental and physical damage while possessing a person."

The mayor's expression indicated she wasn't happy Francine and Penny had essentially admitted what they were. Maybe it was one crisis too many for Oldham. What if she accused them of lying?

Guilt plagued Francine. How the hell were they going to protect the entire town and stop the Apocalypse if no one believed them?

"Which of you killed the demon inside of Rimmon?" Chief Wright asked.

"I did," Penny said. "It was holding my daughter hostage."

"But Rimmon was alive when I tucked him into his bed at his condo and locked up the place Tuesday night," Francine interjected.

"So you all lied to me and my partner that night," Pence sneered.

Francine stepped around Neal. "Like you wouldn't have kept every single person at Java's Palace under a forty-eight-hour psych hold if they'd told you the truth Tuesday night?"

"Can you please stop the pointless bickering?" the older woman beside the mayor snapped. "We've got dead rising in the surrounding states now, and according to the other Red Cross regions, it's spreading like crazy across those. We don't have enough spaces to house all these people. Not to mention, some of those risen people are cracking under the stress of what's happened to them. We are running out of spaces in the mental health care facilities, too."

"And you are?" Francine drawled.

"Irene Campbell, director of the Northern Illinois Region of the American Red Cross." Her scowl deepened. "If you are two of the Four Horsemen—"

"Soccer Moms," Francine corrected.

"What?" Mrs. Campbell stared at Francine like she'd lost her last marble. Or they both had.

"We prefer being called the Soccer Moms of the Apocalypse," Penny added with a grin. "We definitely aren't men."

"Furthermore, we are all mothers, our kids play on the same soccer team, and we all drive minivans. So, yes, we are the Soccer Moms of the Apocalypse." Francine finished.

"Besides, it's better branding," Neal said.

"Branding?" Mayor Oldham blurted. "We're in the middle of a crisis, and you people are worried about branding?"

Everyone in the room ignored her.

"All right, then." Mrs. Campbell crossed her arms, but her voice was a bit calmer. "Can you tell me when the dead are going to stop crawling out of their graves? We do not have the resources to care for them all."

"We don't know," Francine answered. "It's not like the Almighty gave us an instruction manual when He decided to make us the Soccer Moms."

"Then you need to find out." Mayor Oldham didn't sound angry. More like she was grasping at any straw she could find in the maelstrom. "Have you contacted any of the local religious leaders? Hell, I can contact the Archbishop of Chicago for you if that's what it takes."

"Actually—" Francine started.

"This is ridiculous!" Pence waved his arms. "The Four Horsemen bring the Apocalypse! We stop this by killing them!" He pointed at Francine and Penny.

"The Four Soccer Moms," Gene said. "And you might want to read your Bible, Officer. They are the servants of Christ."

"Maybe that's what you believe," Pence sneered.

"I'm an atheist, Officer Pence," Gene said coolly. "I believe in facts. Fact one is my wife is Pestilence, a Soccer Mom of the Apocalypse and according to the Book of Revelation, her appearance breaks the first Seal of the Apocalypse. Fact two is that three other women I know exhibit the abilities of the other three Horsemen, or as they prefer Soccer Moms. Fact three is the dead are rising, which indicates the fifth Seal has broken. All of these changes my opinion on the possible existence of God."

At the look of adoration for her husband on Penny's face, Francine knew the Hudsons would find a way for their marriage to survive.

Assuming they all could get through this meeting.

"Chief Wright, perhaps you need to have a talk with Officer Pence before he says something that will get the department sued for discrimination." Francine scowled at them both.

The chief took the hint. "Officer Pence, why don't you step outside, grab a cup of coffee, and get some fresh air?"

He opened his mouth, but from the expression on the chief's face, he decided against whatever he was going to say. With a quick pivot, he stomped out of the principal's office, slamming the door behind him.

"How do I prevent my people from getting possessed, ladies?" Chief

Wright rocked on his heels. "This weirdness with the dead is bad enough without half my department working against the other half."

"We need something for everyone," the mayor added. "We've already got guys like Hank and Billy Eastwood running around town, armed to the teeth and claiming zombies are going to eat everyone's brains. If this demon thing gets out, someone's going to end up dead."

Francine shook her head. "Then you probably shouldn't have sent Pence out of the room."

"Why?" the chief asked.

Francine resisted the urge to roll her eyes. "He was ready to join the vigilantes last night at the cemetery."

Chapter 25

Francine tried not to smirk as Chief Wright let out a string of obscenities that would have sent her mother straight for the super-sized bottle of dish soap. "Graham, get Pence back here!"

"Yes, sir." Not a muscle on the officer's face twitched, but there was a definite twinkle in his eye as he left the principal's office. Graham made a point of gently closing the door behind him.

"First of all, we can keep everyone home," Francine said. "There are symbols we can paint over doors and windows to protect the inhabitants."

"What about businesses?" Mayor Oldham asked.

"According to our sources, we can't use protection symbols on businesses, hospitals, or anything else that's considered a public place." Francine gestured to include the high school.

"We thought churches were safe, but two demons attacked Father Perez and his assistant at Saint Michael's," Penny added.

"Is he your religious contact?" Chief Wright raised an eyebrow.

"Not at first." Francine chuckled. "I was running into a bunch of dead ends in my research, so Penny went to see the father on the off chance he knew something we hadn't thought of. However, the pastor at my family's church has volunteered to help us as well."

"So, the two guys with the rap sheets who beat up the padre and Mrs. Cordero were possessed?" An incredulous look filled the police chief's face.

"Yes," Penny said firmly.

"An attack on you I can understand," Mayor Oldham said. "But why Father Perez?"

"They didn't want him to notify the Vatican. They have specialists who handle demon incursions." Francine gestured in the general direction of the Catholic church.

"The demons' real problem as far as Oakfield goes is my dad used to be a lay forensic accountant for Vatican City," Gene continued. "Even if they'd managed to silence the padre, Dad knew the right people to call for this type of pest control."

"I don't recall ever seeing you at mass." The mayor smirked.

"Like I said, I'm an atheist, and my family was not Catholic," Gene retorted. "Dad only worked for them."

"Never mind the church gossip," Chief Wright grumbled. "How do we know who's possessed and who's not?"

"It takes some training—" Gene started.

"Thank you, Mr. Hudson, but I'd like to hear the answer from Heaven's professionals." The mayor gestured at Francine and Penny.

"It's harder for non-Soccer Mom people to spot a possessed person." Francine shrugged. "The best explanation is the face looks too long, the eyes too far apart or too close together, and it may look like something's crawling under the person's skin."

"That's not a lot to go on," Chief Wright said.

"What if we have a Vatican demon hunter teach your officers how to identify a possessed person?" Francine said.

"Demon hunters?" The mayor rolled her eyes. "You expect me to believe the Mother Church has people who—"

Trying not to laugh, Francine looked at Penny. Even Gene and Neal wore matching smirks as Mayor Oldham worked through who the specialists were and what they did.

"You just told us your father was a forensic accountant." Mayor Oldham scowled at Gene.

He shrugged. "How do you think they tracked the demons? It's not all levitation and head-spinning. They don't want the public's attention any more than the Mob does."

"Ms. Coy-Astin, I'll take you up on your offer." Chief Wright nodded sharply. "Any edge would be helpful."

"Can these demons possess the newly risen?" Mrs. Campbell asked. "I don't want my staff and volunteers at risk."

At Penny's hesitation, Francine plunged ahead. "We don't know. Technically, they can't possess a corpse, but no one's sure what will happen with a resurrected person. The risen are God's Chosen, and they have souls, but we can't rely on the assumption they are immune from demons."

"What about you four?" Chief Wright asked.

Francine smiled. "We sing a lot of show tunes to keep our minds an inhospitable environment for the demons."

Mayor Oldham's expression turned thoughtful. "That actually makes sense." She turned to Mrs. Campbell. "What if we piped Broadway soundtracks through the school's PA system?"

The Red Cross director nodded. "Sounds like a good idea during the waking hours. It might drive everyone a little crazy at night though." She shook her head. "Our real problem is we're already packed to the gills here. With opening the middle schools as shelters, I'm running out of people to man the schools."

"Pastor Burns at First Methodist is already taking in former parishioners as is Father Perez at Saint Michael's. What if we ask citizens to take in some of the overflow?" Francine suggested. "Those who volunteer extra beds and couches will have first priority in getting their homes painted with protection symbols."

"I don't know." The mayor tapped her index finger against her lips before she added, "Some people aren't going to be happy with the woo-woo aspect."

"If they have dead people sleeping at their house, I don't think they're going to have problems with occult sigils in black light paint," Francine said dryly.

"Why UV paint?" Chief Wright asked.

"So people don't get freaked out by the woo-woo aspect," Neal said dryly.

"We can use any type of paint," Penny said. "Or even Sharpies if we're desperate according to my father-in-law."

"Can you draw them for us?" The mayor walked over and grabbed a few sheets of paper from the printer tray. "We can make copies and distribute them."

"So you can tell all the demons in Oakfield we poor mortals are on to them?" Chief Wright wore an incredulous expression as he looked at Mayor Oldham.

"What makes you think the demons aren't following the Soccer Moms already?" she pointed out.

"They are," Francine said. "Something else you need to keep in mind is demons are intangible in their normal form. They look like black smoke, and they act like it, which means they can get into any place that's not airtight."

Officer Graham burst into the principal's office. "Chief! Pence is gone. He tore off out of the parking lot in his patrol car. Simmons said he was muttering something about the Eastwood brothers having the right idea about putting the dead back in their graves."

Francine pinched the bridge of her nose as Famine tried to break free. That's all they needed. A bunch of vigilantes blasting away at the righteous dead would definitely cause a public panic.

Chapter 26

Francine turned to Penny. "Where are Winona and Dee?" She wasn't about to hand over Wila and Dani's real identities to the mayor and chief of police. She had no idea of how they were going to use their knowledge about her and Penny in the long run.

"They were going to their respective churches to collect donations and bring them over to the high school." Penny was careful not to say Wila was still at work. The city couldn't afford to lose a paramedic. Not in the middle of this mess.

Francine pulled her phone out of her tote pocket and checked the time. "They could be here and gone by now." She texted the possible vigilante issue with Pence going off half-cocked to Wila and Dani, but the drumbeat of power inside her made it hard to concentrate.

"You know Pence will charge us with assaulting an officer if we lay a hand on him," Penny protested.

"Not if I deputize you ladies." A slight smile tilted the corners of the chief's mouth.

"I'll call Karen for a ride home for me and Gene and to pick up Brittany," Neal said. "You two need to find Pence and the Eastwood brothers before they do something really stupid."

"Apologize to Jermaine, Sherlyn, and the boys for me." Francine gave her husband a peck on the lips. "I'll be home as soon as I can."

She darted past Officer Graham and out the door before Famine's power burst from her. Penny jogged beside her, her clothes fading to white and her crown manifesting on her hair as they headed for the back hallway be-hind the gym. No sense in scaring the Red Cross staff or their charges.

Jingling came from behind them. Francine slowed and looked over her shoulder. Officer Graham ran to catch up with them.

"What's wrong, Officer?" Francine stopped, and Penny pulled up short and turned around to rejoin her.

Graham blinked and drew back at the changes in their appearances. But he collected himself and straightened his spine. "The chief prefers me and Simmons accompany you ladies. He wants to make sure Pence knows you have his backing."

"What about your partner?" Francine said.

"There's a reason I don't normally have one on patrol and Pence does." He grinned. "But if you don't mind, allow me to lead the way so you don't get yourselves shot."

He strode toward the end of the corridor and turned the corner. Francine and Penny followed. Two armed police stood at the end of the second hallway in front of the double doors. If Francine had charged around the corner, looking as she did right now, they would surely have opened fire. Even with Graham's presence, the pair of cops reached for their sidearms at the sight of the two Soccer Moms of the Apocalypse.

"At ease," Graham barked. "These woman have been deputized by Chief Wright. Got a problem with it, take your complaint up with him."

Both police officers backed into the opposing walls as Francine and Penny strode past them. Francine made a point of smiling at the officer on her left. The smell of urine flooded the air, and a dark spot appeared on the front of his pants.

When they stepped outside into the student parking lot, Graham held up his index finger. "I'll be right back with Simmons. Please don't take off without us."

Once he disappeared around the corner of the brick building, Penny whispered, "Have you picked up Wila's insane sense of humor? You didn't have to literally scare the piss out of that cop inside."

"I guess I'm so used to using my looks to get what I want," Francine teased. The truth of her statement hit hard even as she said it. This was different than before, wasn't it? Fear was a much different prod than desire and attraction, right? She sighed. "You're right. I'll watch myself."

"All I'm saying is stopping the Apocalypse will be hard enough without frightening the very people we are supposed to save. Or whose help we may need."

"I got it," Francine snapped.

Penny's irritation filled her face. "No breakfast?"

"Not enough breakfast." Francine sighed. "I was going to pick up Long Johns on the way home after dropping off the boxes of food and bags of clothes."

Penny pulled her phone out of her fur-lined cape.

Francine cocked her head. "How'd you do that?"

"You're not the only one playing with their powers." Penny smiled as she texted. "Technically, our Horsemen personas act like how your sorority sister explained our horses. Our phones, bags, and civilian clothes are still here, just in a side dimension."

A police SUV braked beside the sidewalk to Francine's left. Graham rolled down Simmons' window and grinned. "Can I offer you ladies a ride?'

On the other hand, poor Simmons looked absolutely terrified.

"Thank you, but we've got our own." Francine raised her forefinger and thumb to her lips and blew a piercing whistle. Sable and Silver galloped around the corner of the high school, but there was no sound of their hooves striking the dormant turf. She never realized how quiet their steeds were until now.

"We need to make a quick stop by Saint Michael's," Penny said. "Father Perez will have some special supplies for both you gentlemen and for us in case we run into demons."

Graham nodded. "Whatever you think is best. Dispatch is tracking Pence's patrol car as we speak. So far, he's headed in the direction of his house. 15397 County Road 57."

"For now, stay with us." Francine climbed onto Sable's back and patted her neck. "You heard Pestilence, baby. Saint Michael's, but keep it slow so the police can keep up."

The horse tossed her ebony mane and started off in, what was for her, an easy canter. Silver pranced beside her. Francine glanced over her shoulder. Graham drove behind them. At least, he wasn't crazy enough to have his siren blaring though he did turn on the flashing lights. Between the extremely few automobiles on the road and the traffic lights programmed to allow emergency vehicles clearance through the intersections, nothing impeded their progress.

When they charged into the Saint Michael's parking lot a few minutes later, Dani's minivan sat next to Father Perez's tiny hatchback, a forty-year-old sedan, and a scarlet and gray pickup that seemed familiar. If Francine remembered correctly, it was one of the trucks blocking the entrance to the Oakfield Cemetery last night. The moment Sable and Silver's hooves touched the church's land, the minivan shivered and shifted into Verde. When they reached Dani's mare, the three horses nuzzled each other in greeting.

Francine slid from Sable's back and stroked her nose. "Ladies, we need you to turn back to minivans. We don't want to tip off any demons who might drive by that we're here."

Sable snorted, but she trotted over to an open parking spot and shifted back into a vehicle. The other two horses followed suit. However, Graham parked on the other side of Father Perez's hatchback.

"Dani's back in the community center." Penny strode in that direction. Once again, she was dressed in jeans and her University of Chicago hoodie.

Francine looked down. Yep, her clothes were back to normal, too. Jeans. Sweater. She tugged the cotton knit at her throat. Yep, even her turtleneck was back. She looked back at the two police officers. "You guys coming?"

Graham shook his head as he tentatively approached her. "How do you do that?"

"Do what?" she asked innocently.

"You know what I mean," he growled.

Simmons followed his fellow officer. "Thanks for not looking like the starving, scary person at Java's Palace on Tuesday night."

"You're welcome." It seemed to be a better answer than the truth. She'd left to return the very human Seth Rimmon to his condo. More guilt gnawed at her soul. She should have stayed with Rimmon Tuesday night. Or taken him to a hospital. She could have stopped the demons from killing him. Either way, maybe he could have been saved.

She turned and headed for the community center. The center had been built in the nineteen-fifties on the land between the church proper and the rectory after the membership outgrew the original basement. It connected the other two buildings so the priests didn't have to deal with inclement weather as well as providing a venue for other programs.

Penny waited by the doors. "Is it just me or do you notice something odd about the parking lot?"

Francine looked behind her. "No one's dropping off supplies or picking them up." She turned back to her friend. "Not to compare, but my church was a lot busier."

"So was the Presbyterian church when we swung by." Penny frowned.

"We're not going to find out by standing out in the cold." Francine reached for the handle and yanked the door open.

They entered the center. The majority of noise came from the center's gymnasium to their right. Francine followed Penny in that direction.

Like the high school, there were cots lined up on tarps used to protect the basketball court's polished hardwood. Unlike the high school, only half of them showed signs of use. But the people here looked less traumatized. In fact, they looked more like they were here for Bible study and recreation.

An elderly nun in a full habit approached them. "May I assist you? Do you need a place to find succor in these end times?"

Another man walked up. "They aren't from the graveyard, Sister Dorothy. Why don't you go back to reading stories to the children?"

She smiled up at him. "Of course, Constable." She tottered back toward a group of kids in the corner of the gym. Some lounged on the colorful pillows. Others tried to sit very properly.

The man who diverted the nun was dressed in modern clothes, but his brilliant red moustache dipped before it connected with his equally red sideburns, the style giving away how long ago he had passed. He wore a rueful expression. "The sister didn't quite come back all the way from Heaven. We've got to keep her occupied. I'm Clarence O'Leary, former police captain of Oakfield. What can I do assist my fellow law enforcement officers?"

He held out his huge hand to Graham, ignoring Francine and Penny.

Simmons's dark complexion turned an ashy hue. "Captain O'Leary?"

However, Graham shook the risen man's hand. "A pleasure to meet you, Captain, but Mrs. Coy-Astin and Mrs. Hudson outrank me and Simmons. You should speak directly to them."

"My apologies, ladies." O'Leary inclined his head and smiled underneath the massive amount of facial hair. "I'm still getting used to this new century."

"It's all right, Captain." Francine returned his smile. "Sometimes, the men of this century forget as well." Her stomach chose that moment to rumble.

Loud enough, the gentlemen playing chess at a nearby table turned to stare out her.

"We were supposed to meet with Father Perez and—" Francine grimaced as her stomach rumbled even louder.

"You okay?" Penny eyed her.

"No," Francine whispered. She was losing control of Famine. The stomachs of the police surrounding her started growling, too. "Get me to the kitchen before I lose total control."

Penny wrapped an arm around Francine's waist. She could feel her skin tighten as Penny rushed her past the cots and toward another set of doors. Penny kept her upright, but it was Francine's nose that found the kitchen.

Long Johns.

Perfect white boxes of deep fried rectangles of dough, stuffed with the most delectable vanilla crème, and thick chocolate frosting.

She started eating.

Her skin loosened.

She could think again.

Francine looked up to see everyone in the community center dining room, including Penny, Dani, and the cops, staring at her in horror.

Chapter 27

"What?" Francine said around a mouthful of dough, crème, and frosting. "I'm starving."

"Dammit, Francine!" Dani literally stomped her foot. "You know you can't skip meals!"

Francine swallowed. "I didn't think I was going to get dragged into a manhunt for a rogue cop this morning." She shoved more Long John into her mouth.

"You are so paying me back for those damn doughnuts," Dani hissed.

All the men except the two priests stared at Francine like she was crazy. She looked at the empty boxes surrounding her.

Or maybe they stared because she wolfed down four dozen Long Johns in a few seconds. Yep, she definitely owed Dani for the doughnuts. And the weird part was she didn't feel a bit sick to her stomach.

Francine examined her sticky fingers. "How about I go wash up?"

"No," Penny said firmly. "You need to finish the final two boxes. Last thing we need is you losing control while we bring in Pence and his friends."

"Father Perez, do you have any high protein and high carb snacks we can take with us?" Dani asked.

"No!" Francine snapped. "I'm not taking food from the people here who need it."

"Dani's right." Father Perez stalked into the kitchen itself and returned with a large bag of trail mix. "Take this with you."

"I can't—" Francine held up a hand.

"Yes, you can." Father Perez scowled at her. "If not for saving the world, take it so you don't accidentally cause the mere mortals around you to starve to death."

"All right." Francine nodded. "Point taken, Father."

"Good." There was a strong hint of satisfaction in his voice as he handed the bag to Dani.

"You pull your curse upon yourself so you don't inflict it on others?" The dark-haired man in an apron who spoke seemed familiar . . .

The man who knelt before her in the Oakfield Cemetery last night. He was with Hank Eastwood.

"I'm sorry." She smiled up at him. "We weren't formally introduced last night."

"Lucas Manewell." He looked a bit uncomfortable.

"Sorry for not shaking your hand," she said. "I'm normally not so messy when I eat."

"Finish your Long Johns, Lady Famine." He turned to Father Perez. "I'll start the lunch prep, Father." Lucas strode into the kitchen.

Father McAvoy eyed her. "You seem to have made an impression on Mr. Manewell."

"Not exactly the one I wanted to make," she said sourly as she reached for the fifth box of Long Johns and opened it. Disappointed, she looked up at Dani. "Vanilla?"

"The Bake Shoppe was already out of maple, and you just inhaled the last of the chocolate they had." Dani shook her head. "Seems like everyone in town decided on doughnuts this morning. They think the world is ending."

"Let me finish eating and get cleaned up." Francine picked up a white-frosted Long John. "Then we'll hit the road."

👆   💀   👆

Dani and Penny followed Francine to the ladies' room in the community center. Penny filled Dani in on this morning's events at the high school while Francine washed the sugary residue from her hands and face, used the facilities, and washed her hands again.

"Wila plans to take her grandmother to the Hudsons when she gets off duty," Dani said. "She'll sleep there this afternoon. In the meantime, Edward is guarding the kids while I came down to help Father Perez. The Corderos are supposed to be here in a few minutes, then I can leave."

"If you come with us, you're going to expose yourself to the mayor and police chief as a Soccer Mom of the Apocalypse." Francine yanked a couple of paper towels from the dispenser and dried her hands. "We have no idea how they might use the information against us."

Penny laughed. "Are you kidding? Verde confirmed her identity when we rode onto the church property."

"I'm counting on Graham and Simmons to be unnerved enough they didn't notice or they've forgotten Verde's plate number." Francine wiped the water from between her fingers.

"Dani, it might be better if you go back to my house," Penny said. "Since the demons are attacking our homes—"

Francine tossed her paper towels into the trash and leaned her hip against the counter. "Taking me out last night was just the cherry for the demons who possessed my neighbors. They wanted Laura and Rose."

Penny threw her hands in the air. "But we still have no idea why the demons want the resurrected folks."

Dani hugged herself. "That means any and all of the shelters will be the demons' next target."

"Which is why we suggested placing the risen in people's homes and painting the symbols to protect the living and the dead," Francine said.

"But we can't figure out their plan until we know why the demons want them," Penny said.

Francine chewed in her bottom lip until the right inquiry presented itself amidst the sugar-high in her brain. "Actually, the better question is why didn't the demons head straight for my basement once Karen and I got them out of my neighbors' bodies. They could have possessed Neal, Laura, and Rose without any problem."

"Except my mother-in-law knows how to deal with the darn things," Penny said.

"No, Francine's on to something." Dani drummed her right fingers against her left arm. "What if they can't possess the righteous dead? What if there is something a human loses at death that not even God can restore"

"I doubt if it's that easy of an answer," Penny said.

"Then, we need to go pick the brains of a couple of priests," Francine said.

Chapter 28

The three Soccer Moms rejoined the police and the priests in the dining room.

"Officers, could you excuse us for a minute or two?" Francine smiled politely at the policemen. "We've got a couple of questions for Fathers Perez and McAvoy."

"Must that include me?" O'Leary asked. "Unfortunately, I have a bit of experience with spiritualists in my day."

Father McAvoy cleared his throat. "I already told Mr. O'Leary a bit of what was happening and what I used to do for the Church." He gestured at the other two officers. "Since these two gentlemen are accompanying you, I assume they are not possessed?"

"No, they aren't," Francine said. "But in the future, please don't make that assumption. That's how Edward ruined our plan to pump the demon inside Seth Rimmon for information."

"Maybe Mr. O'Leary and Officers Graham and Simmons could have some insight into our questions," Dani interjected.

Francine shot her a dirty look. It wasn't like Dani had to stay at the Cellar and help Wila after Edward threw holy water on a possessed attorney. The awful burns on the attorney's face and scalp still haunted Francine's nightmares. She was rather grateful Mr. Treeger's burns from Karen's holy water balloon were comparatively mild.

"Fine, but first, we need some holy water for the officers to carry," Francine said.

"I'll get the holy water." With an amused expression, Father Perez sauntered out of the dining room.

Father McAvoy poked the nose piece of his glasses. "Now, what were your questions, ladies?"

Penny reiterated the issues they had discussed in the women's bathroom. The priest's blank look didn't inspire any confidence.

"I honestly don't know if the recently risen can be possessed or why the demons might want them." He turned and settled in the closest chair. "When Dani told me about the attack at Francine's house last night, I made some calls, including the cardinal currently in charge of the taskforce and the Holy Father himself."

Father McAvoy shook his head. "Other than the ten resurrections mentioned in the Bible, including Christ Himself, there's no evidence of demons possessing them or even trying to abduct them."

"But all of those incidents were cases of one person being raised from the dead at a time," Francine said. "Including Christ. You can't consider the Apocalypse an average Biblical resurrection."

"No, it isn't," he admitted.

"So what about when innocent people were targeted by demons in the Bible?" Penny crossed her arms. "Francine and I have read the Good Book forwards and backwards. All of the incidents regarding demons are typical possessions. They're exorcised by invoking God, just like you guys do. We need some insight, Padre."

"I wish I had the insight to give you ladies." Father McAvoy shook his head. "I may have been called to serve, but I'm still a mere mortal. God has granted you gifts beyond my capacity to even truly understand." A weak smile crossed his face. "I wish I had the answers to give you. I truly wish I did."

Father Perez strode back into the dining room, carrying medium-sized brown paper bags with twine handles. "I've got plastic squirt bottles. I know it's not the same as water balloons . . ." With growing concern on his face, he looked at each person in turn. "What's wrong?"

"Nothing." Francine chewed on her lower lip before she added. "Except we're on our own, and we have no clue of what we're doing."

The Soccer Moms divided the majority of the squirt bottles between the two police officers and kept one each for themselves. Simmons didn't look too sure about the clear plastic, but Graham pointed out the bottles gave them a lot more control than, say, a water balloon.

In the meantime, Mr. O'Leary gathered a couple of the risen who had all their marbles and a few extra IQ points so the priests could start teaching them how to fight demons. Father McAvoy finally admitted that his morning discussion with Rome resulted in no additional help coming to Oakfield as well as no information.

Francine's phone rang, and she check the ID. Neal. She stepped away from the group. "Hi, honey."

"Hey, babe. Please tell me you got some more breakfast."

She chuckled. "I owe Dani the money for six dozen boxes of Long Johns."

Neal whistled. "Things are that bad, huh?"

"Yeah."

"The Richards and Mr. Treeger are here. I'm going to make lunch for them." He hesitated for a moment. "Is it okay if Karen and Laura go ahead and fill them in on the real situation?"

"I take it Mr. Treeger has remembered more of what happened last night."

"It didn't help when Korbin and Kirby started blabbing about you, your superpowers, and your magic horse."

Francine laughed. She couldn't help herself. "Yeah, I guess the ladies need to come clean with our neighbors. Have you talked to Brittany?"

"Yes, and Wila. Gene said it was okay for her to stay at the Hudsons' house. Between him, Wila, and Edward, they've got the kids covered.

"Damn." Francine chuckled. "You know Wila will be demanding a lot of pool time next summer."

"She can live in the friggin' pool if it means keeping our daughter safe."

Francine's heart swelled with affection. "I'll be home as soon as I can."

"Be careful, babe. You already know Pence has a few screws loose."

"I will. I love you."

"Back at you."

She disconnected the call. After her initial panic at getting filmed turning into Famine, it seemed she was throwing any and all secrecy out the window. Maybe, just maybe, it was for the best.

Chapter 29

This time, Graham and Simmons led the way in their patrol SUV with lights flashing, but the siren silent. Francine and her sisters followed on their steeds. The horses had no problem keeping up with the vehicle. In fact, she had the impression Sable could easily outrun an Indy car.

Francine could feel eyes on them from the surrounding houses as they rode past. If only the people who watched understood the Soccer Moms of the Apocalypse were trying to save them. Maybe they did. No one interfered with them, much less exited their homes.

Their group headed south, out into Illinois farm country. Many of the fields were empty, except for the corn rows. The wet fall had delayed harvesting the ears.

The highway was just as empty as the fields for the most part. The odder thing were the folks both living and recently risen who tailgated in the local cemeteries. Good. Not everyone was taking potshots at the rising dead. But then, the small township graveyards were filled with families who'd farmed this area for generations. The living glanced curiously at the patrol car, but the newly risen stared at the three women on horseback.

Could the living not see the Soccer Moms? Their behavior reminded Francine of their ride through town on Tuesday to rescue Penny's daughter Justine. Most of the pedestrians and drivers ignored them, but a handful of others took notice of the Soccer Moms passing by. Maybe it was just some of the living who could see Francine and her friends in their alternate forms.

Graham signaled a right turn onto County Road 57. Now, he needed to stick to the plan. As soon as the thought passed through Francine's mind, Graham killed the flashing red and blue lights when his official SUV completed the maneuver.

"Let's go cross country, Sable."

Her horse leapt over the drainage ditch that paralleled the county road and took off at full speed across a harvested soy bean field. Sable's hooves rustled the dead leaves and stems in her passage. Silver and Verde raced on either side of her.

They jumped over fences and dodged trees while they crossed field after field. Wind tugged on the ragged edges of Francine's robes and whistled in her ears. The overcast sky leeched whatever color was left on the planet. No one would ever suspect it was close to noon from the darkness.

Pence's house was ahead. A ranch home with white siding and black shutters, except for a redwood deck and a glass-encased Florida room at the back of the house.

They needed to approach the house unseen. The east side of the house didn't have any windows at all. It probably was the garage. Francine nudged Sable's ribs with her knee, and the horse turned to her left. The other two horses and riders followed suit.

The acre of grass around the home and the two matching out buildings had yellowed with the cooling of the season. Naked trees marked the western perimeter of the property. An Oakfield Police Department SUV sat in the driveway behind a red pickup. A second truck, electric blue on a raised frame, was parked next to the red one.

"The blue pickup looks like one of the trucks Laura and I saw at the cemetery last night," Francine said. "It could be one of the Eastwood brothers' vehicles."

"How do we know if Pence is inside the house?" Penny frowned. "He may have left with one of the other vigilantes. And if he is in there, who else is in there with him?"

"The last thing we need is an innocent getting injured or killed if somebody inside decides to open fire," Dani said.

The horses slowed until a copse of trees on the adjoining property shielded them. It was too damn quiet. The police SUV carrying Graham and Simmons rolled to a stop behind the slight rise before the county road flowed past Pence's front yard.

Francine glanced to her right. Penny's white cloak still draped her shoulders, but instead of white leather, she wore gold and silver armor. A matching helmet replaced her crown.

A shiver ran through Francine. She and Dani only wore tattered robes. Even if they switched to their jeans and sweaters, the cotton wouldn't give them any more protection from bullets if Pence decided to be stupid. That was the whole reason they told Graham and Simmons to stay back.

Maybe if Wila and Penny could change their outfits, she could, too.

Francine concentrated. When she opened her eyes, black, matte scales covered her scrawny body, yet they moved with her.

Both Penny and Dani laughed.

"This isn't funny. Pence is a cop. He's armed, and Hank Eastwood was last night, so we've got to assume he's armed today. Besides, Penny's already wearing armor." Francine turned to Dani. "Aren't you afraid of being shot?"

Dani shoved back her hood. A skull with glowing green eye sockets grinned back at Francine. "What makes you think I have any vital organs to hit? Or that I have a life to take? I had to die on Wila's kitchen floor to become what I am." Dani faced Pence's house again and pulled up her hood. "I'm not pursuing it, but I never feared it either since it meant seeing Heath again."

"What if someone not involved in Pence's stupidity is inside the house?" Francine said. "Do we let them get shot?"

"We won't know who's inside the house until we check. Shall we get this over with, ladies?" Penny urged Silver forward.

Their horses passed through or around the split rail fence guarding

Pence's property line, depending on the branch of physics Francine adhered to according to her sorority sister Gretchen. It still gave Francine the willies. They rode toward the garage. If Pence had cameras or motion detectors set up around his place, the Soccer Moms were already screwed.

"Anyone else feeling that?" Dani asked when they were halfway across the dormant grass.

The unmistakable sensation itched beneath Francine's scaly armor. "Demons."

"Inside the house," Penny added.

"I'll take the front," Dani said. "You two take the back."

"Are you insane?" Francine blurted. "You're going to scare the piss out of whoever's inside."

"Says the Soccer Mom who deliberately made a cop pee his pants at the high school for no reason other than spite," Penny said.

"I plan to cause enough confusion you guys can come in the back without anyone getting hurt." Dani's cackle sounded like dice rattling in a Yahtzee cup. "Except the demons, of course." She urged Verde into a trot as the pair headed for the front door.

"When she's Death, does her voice ever freak you out?" Francine whispered as she and Penny guided their horses toward the redwood deck at the back of the house.

"It's better than your Marilyn Monroe with pneumonia wheeze."

"Hey!"

Penny merely grinned at her.

The flowerbeds lining the back of the house had been cleaned, weeded, and mulched in preparation for winter. The meticulous care didn't make sense for a man's man like Pence. If he gardened for relaxation, it sure wasn't making a dent in his anger issues. But according to Simmons, Pence wasn't married, didn't have a girlfriend, and didn't have any kids.

Shades had been pulled, and curtains had been drawn on all the windows at the back of the house, except the Florida room. But through the windows of the seasonal retreat, Francine could see the door to the rest of the house was closed. Yet, she would have sworn they were being watched. If she and her sisters sensed the demons, surely the demons knew the Soccer Moms were outside the house in return.

She lifted her right foot from the stirrup, but Penny grabbed her arm.

"Sable and Silver can get us inside without breaking the windows or doors."

Francine snorted but stayed in her saddle. "Did you not look at the pictures I texted you of my kitchen after last night's demon attack?"

Sable turned her head and glared at Francine with one midnight black eye. Penny snickered, and Silver made an amused *whuff*.

"All I'm saying is don't stay inside this house once you drop me off." Francine leaned forward and patted her horse's neck. "I can't afford to have Pence sue me for the property damage."

Sable shook her head, jingling her tack.

"If I can handle five demons in my own kitchen, I can handle a couple inside Pence's," Francine murmured.

Sable pawed the dormant grass, her answer clear. She'd go along with the plan, but she sure didn't like it.

Francine tensed at the muted sound of a doorbell. From the front of the house, Dani yelled, "Trick or treat!"

Francine and Penny ducked low against their steeds' backs. Sable and Silver leapt as one through the wall and into Pence's house.

Francine slid off Sable and flipped her scales to use the base as a cudgel. Once the horses were clear, she got a better look at the situation. And her heart threatened to crawl up her throat and run outside after her horse.

The man who warned Francine to leave the Oakfield cemetery just last night stood in front of her. But this time, Hank Eastwood held an elderly woman dressed in a pink fuzzy bathrobe and matching slippers by her throat, and a demon perched on his soul.

Chapter 30

"Let her go," Francine demanded. In her peripheral vision, Dani had disarmed Pence while Penny battled the demon inside the kid who had been spotting the rising dead with binoculars at the cemetery last night.

Of course. The demons would feed on the vigilantes' fear. Except Pence wasn't possessed. Neither was the elderly woman, who was doing her best not to fall apart while the demon squeezed her windpipe.

"I said let her go," Francine repeated.

"Now why would I do that?" The demon inside Hank Eastwood snickered. "I have a bargaining chip, and I'm facing the weakest Horseman."

Of course, it wanted to get under her skin.

"You sure about that?" She took an experimental swing with her scales.

"You have no real weapon to kill me while I'm inside this petty mortal. And your powers merely cause a slow, agonizing death in humans." The demon chuckled. "I'll rip off this bitch's head long before my current pet dies of hunger."

It said all the ugly things that ran through the back of her mind since she and her friends had learned they were the Soccer Moms of the Apocalypse. She had been useless in the battle against Seth Rimmon and his minions. She couldn't have handled the five demons in her house last night without Sable and Karen's help.

But there was one bit of logic he hadn't touched upon. All she had to do was get him to release the woman. She lowered her scales, slipped her hand into the pocket in her armor, and grabbed her squirt bottle.

"If I'm so inept, why do you need a hostage?" she mocked. "A big, bad demon such as yourself could easily best me."

"I might beat you, but I need her to kill you."

"I won't kill anyone for you," the hostage wheezed, anger in her hazel eyes.

Francine's sight shifted. The woman was one of the risen from the pale blue diamond clarity of her soul. The bastards had come after a lone elderly woman, who probably had no clue of what was going on like so many of the recently risen.

"Oh, darling." The demon licked the side of the woman's face while keeping its eyes on Francine. The older woman cringed at the saliva smeared across her cheek "I didn't say you would do the actual killing."

Francine raised her squirt bottle, thumbed off the top, and squeezed. The demon jerked the woman upward by the throat. She flailed and kicked because she couldn't breathe. Most of the holy water struck the woman, but some of the water hit the demon's fingers. A sizzling sound was accompanied by the awful stench of burning flesh. Skin peeled off the demon's fingers.

But this demon didn't scream. Instead, he smiled, a horrible rictus that made Dani's skull look positively benign. A couple of the light ribbons holding the elderly woman's soul in place broke. Energy flowed from the risen woman's soul into Hank's body. The look on the demon's face was pure ecstasy as the pale blue of her soul darkened. Her eyes rolled back in her head.

Francine took a step towards them and shifted her scales to swing at the demon's knees. She needed to knock it away from its victim, but a sick feeling washed over her, more like extreme morning sickness instead of the gnawing hunger of her alter ego. She tried to take another step. Her strength faltered, and she dropped her scales.

"What on earth—" She couldn't move. The demon inside Hank Eastwood seemed to be using the power of the risen woman's soul to entrap Francine.

No, not trap her. Kill her.

"Sable!"

Her mare phased back into the house and let out an awful scream of terror. The same terror washing over Francine.

"Sable! Get out!" Dani yelled. "We've got it!"

Francine's heart ripped when her horse collapsed on Pence's kitchen table. The wood gave way under Sable's weight with a series of sickening cracks. She whinnied in agony. The same pain wracked Francine, and she fell to her knees.

The woman's soul fractured. Ebony chips fell from the main jewel. The demon dropped her and focused on Francine. Sable cried out, as the demon turned the soul energy full force on Francine. She was literally being ripped apart inside out.

Dani shoved Pence into a recliner before she rushed the demon struggling with Penny over her bow. With a slash of Dani's scythe, white light flashed, and a tiny wisp of smoke escaped from Billy Eastwood's nostrils before he dropped onto the carpet of the family room.

Freed from the other demon's onslaught, Penny whipped an arrow from her quiver and shot Hank Eastwood in the head. Or rather the demon possessing Hank. Another brilliant flash of light, and Hank fell to the linoleum.

Francine toppled over on her side at the sudden release of the demon's painful grip. All she could see were the eyes of the hostage, her pupils so dilated the hazel irises were no longer visible.

Chapter 31

In the background, Pence shouted, "All of you are under arrest!"

"You still here, Francine?" Dani stood over her.

"You're Death." Francine groaned. Every cell in her body ached. "You tell me."

"I've got you on trespassing, assault with deadly weapons . . ." Pence continued though no one was listening to him.

"Oh, god. Sable?" Francine pushed herself upright.

"She's fine." Dani reached down with a boney hand. Francine grabbed it and let her friend pull her to her feet. "She's outside."

Francine turned. Yep, Sable and Silver both stood on the deck and peered through one of the kitchen windows.

She looked back at Dani. "What the heck just happened?" She couldn't stop the hysterical edge to her voice.

Before Dani had a chance to answer, Penny knelt next to the elderly woman and placed two fingers on the woman's neck. "She doesn't have a pulse. Francine get over here! I need you to do compressions!"

"Get your hands off my grandmother!" Pence's red face, blue eyes, and white-blond hair nearly made him look patriotic. He lunged out of the recliner, his attention fully on Penny and his grandmother. Dani swung her scythe between the officer and the women.

It was a toss-up of whether it was the sharp implement or the animated skeleton with glowing eye sockets that stopped him.

"I-I—" Francine stammered. After watching what the demon had done to the poor lady, fear had grabbed Francine's heart and squeezed it tight.

"Neither of you have the flesh to do mouth-to-mouth, and I don't need Dani's boney fingers to stab holes in the woman's chest," Penny snapped.

"I'll call Graham," Dani said. "He can get paramedics out here faster than I could with 9-1-1."

"Francine!" Penny shouted.

Oh, god. Why did she think she could take care of the other Soccer Moms? This was like watching Dani die in Wila's kitchen all over again.

Moving to the risen woman's side seemed like wading through molasses. Penny had positioned the woman's head face up so she could blow air into the woman's mouth. The wide black pupils stared accusingly at Francine. *Why didn't you save me?*

Francine knelt and started the compressions, calling out the number as she forced the woman's still heart to pump blood. Dani's voice turned into a buzz in the background. Penny pinched the woman's nose shut and breathed into her mouth. Men's voices burred over Dani's. Pence shouted threats. Francine kept counting.

Someone placed a hand on her shoulder. She looked up.

Wila smiled at her, a sad, sympathetic expression. "Hey, girl. Let the pros take over."

"I-I—"

Dani helped Francine to her feet and pulled her away from the body. They were both in jeans and wore their own skin again. Francine tugged on her turtleneck. It was too tight.

Two other EMT teams loaded the Eastwood brothers onto gurneys. Wila questioned Penny over what steps had been taken with the elderly woman before she and her partner Brian arrived on the scene.

The pressure of Francine's turtleneck against her throat and the nausea over what she had witnessed combined. She gagged and choked.

"Outside." Dani pulled her in the direction of the back door.

Once they were on the deck, Francine leaned over the redwood railing and took a deep breath of chill, clean air. The choking sensation disappeared, but not the sick feeling in her gut. Their horses were nowhere in sight, but she could sense Sable within calling distance.

"She's dead."

"I know," Dani whispered.

Francine glared at her. "Dammit, Dani. That lady is more than dead. That demon—"

"I saw what it did."

"How the hell can you be so calm?"

"Because now we know why the demons want the risen dead." At a sharp gust of wind, Dani hugged herself. "I'm just sorry about the price of learning that information."

"Does Wila know the woman's not just dead, but destroyed?" Francine jabbed her forefinger at the house. "Like she never existed?"

"I'm pretty sure she does."

"Then why—" Francine gulped more cold air. "Why is she trying to resuscitate an empty shell?"

"Because she has to." Dani waved a hand in the general direction of where Wila and Brian worked. "She's a paramedic. It's her job unless that woman has a do-not-resuscitate order. Pence claims she's his grandmother, but we don't know that for sure."

"He can be a total jerk, but I don't think he'd lie about his family," Francine said softly.

They stared at the bare branches bobbing in the wind for a long time before Officer Graham opened the door and leaned partway through it. "Ladies? I'm sorry, but if Ms. Coy-Astin has her stomach under control, I need you two to come back inside."

Francine nodded. "I think I'm okay now."

"Good." He nodded and stepped out of the way.

Francine entered the house to a screaming Pence.

"They are evil, Simmons! They killed my grandmother! Arrest them!"

"That's bullshit, and you know it," Simmons muttered.

"You didn't see what she did!" Pence pointed at Francine. "She squirted some kind of acid at Hank and Grandmother!"

Billy Eastwood and the paramedics caring for him were already gone. The second set rolled the gurney carrying Hank Eastwood out the front door. They paused.

The closest EMT eyed Francine suspiciously. "What liquid did you hit our patient and the lady with?"

"Holy water."

The other paramedic burst out laughing. "Told you so, Lee."

His partner made a face. "Let's get this guy to Oakfield Hospital."

They rolled Hank out of the house. Francine silently said a small prayer for Hank to recover from his burns. He wasn't a bad person. He merely let his fear of the rising dead get the better of him.

Penny moved closer to Francine and Dani while the last two paramedics worked on the dead woman.

"Clear!" Wila's partner Brian called out. Everyone else, including Pence, was silent. Wila jerked the oxygen bag out of the way and leaned back.

Brian placed the defibrillator paddles on the risen woman's naked chest. From the looks of things, it hadn't been the first time. The paddles discharged, and her body jerked. The electrocardiograph line remained flat.

Wila placed the mask back over the woman's nose and mouth and squeezed the bag. Brian set the defibrillator to recharge.

"One more," she murmured. "Then we need to call it."

"No, you can't stop!" Pence started on his roll again. "I'll sue you, Ardale! You and the entire Oakfield paramedic squad, you—"

Penny stepped closer to him. "Say it, Officer Pence." She held up her phone. "Let's get it on the record how you really feel about Wila Ardale. You've already threatened legally deputized members of the Oakfield police force. You took an official police vehicle to your home without permission. You allowed a person of interest to hold, according to you, your own grandmother hostage. You—"

"That's enough out of both of you," Graham snapped.

"Clear!" Brian called out again.

Wila jerked the airbag back. Brian applied the paddles and discharged the electricity through them. The woman's body jerked and lay still. The EKG line remained flatter than Francine's pancakes.

"You can't stop. You-you can't. I-I just got her back. Grand-grand-mother—" Pence's shouting turned into broken sobs.

For the first time since she met the officer, Francine felt a tiny pang of sympathy for him.

Chapter 32

Detectives and lab techs from Oakfield came to Pence's house to process the scene and interview the witnesses. Technically, the sheriff's department should have had jurisdiction since Pence's house was outside Oakfield city limits. But the lead detective from Oakfield, a guy named Mason, had a talk with the sheriff when he arrived. Whatever was said between the two men resulted in the sheriff climbing back into his own official SUV and driving away.

From Francine's seat in the living room, she watched the two guys who came to pick up the corpse for the county coroner through the front picture window. The pair sat on the front steps and smoked their cigarettes while the techs did their thing in the kitchen and family room. Penny knew Detective Mason from the whole affair earlier this week with Seth Rimmon, so the detective questioned her first.

Good grief! Had that stupid dinner at The Cellar in Alcott's Steak House only been a week ago?

Dani sat on the couch in Pence's living room, well away from Francine. Simmons sat beside Dani on the couch. Graham had carried in an intact kitchen chair and perched on it. Both patrol officers scribbled notes on their tablets. Everyone ignored Pence, who huddled in his recliner and quietly wept.

Francine was a little envious of Wila. Since she wasn't involved in the whole demon mess, she and Brian had been cleared to leave after their attempts to resuscitate Pence's grandmother failed.

Detective Mason escorted Penny back into Pence's living room. Nothing showed on her face of how the interrogation went. Mason glanced at his notes and looked at Francine. "Ms. Coy-Astin?"

She rose from her chair. Penny passed her and claimed the seat Francine had abandoned. She chewed on her bottom lip as she followed the detective back to the Florida room. The police had to do their jobs, but it would be so easy for the facts to get twisted.

Hell, Pence had been doing his best to twist facts for the last three weeks.

Cold penetrated the glass and framing of Pence's Florida room when Francine entered. She was rather glad she still wore her coat since he hadn't bothered to run heat into the obvious addition.

"Have a seat, ma'am." Mason gestured at one of the white wicker chairs with pink cushions.

The room was far too feminine for Pence. Framed needlepoint sayings hung on the fourth wall. Pink doilies protected both the framed family pictures and the side tables painted white to match the wicker couch and chairs. A basket of yarn sat beside the couch. The beginnings of a crocheted piece with a needle still inserted in a loop guarded the basket. Had he built on this room for his grandmother while she was still alive?

Francine perched on the chair the detective had indicated and clasped her hands on her lap.

Mason sat across from her on the couch. "I'm going to tell you the same thing I told Ms. Hudson. Chief Wright and the mayor told me what you two are. Is Ms. Elante one of the Soccer Moms of the Apocalypse as well?"

"Yes." Francine grimaced at her betrayal of her friend. Dani may hate her, but there was simply no other explanation of why she would be here. Not like the excuse of duty Wila had.

"Why did you bring her into retrieving Pence and his unauthorized borrowing of a city vehicle?"

"Penny and I were concerned demons might be using the vigilantes."

Mason looked up from his note taking. "You mean possessing them?"

"Yes."

"Why?"

"What we would consider negative emotions like anger and fear are catnip to demons." Francine shrugged. "There was a lot of fear coming from the Eastwood brothers along with the other vigilantes last night at the Oakfield Cemetery."

Mason frowned. "What were you doing at the cemetery last night?"

"Penny's dead mother-in-law showed up on Penny's doorstep yesterday morning, and I was running into other people all day who'd recently risen from their graves. Plus, my husband told me some of your fellow police were chasing Jebediah Hauser around downtown while Neal was having a meeting with his sales staff at the Main Street Bistro. So I drove out to the cemetery before sundown to see how many risen we were dealing with."

Mason scribbled in his notebook before he looked up at Francine. "Who accompanied you to the cemetery?"

"Penny's mother-in-law, Laura Hudson."

"The woman who rose from the dead earlier yesterday morning?"

Francine hesitated for a second. Had he asked Penny the same question? "I know this sounds crazy, but the senior Mrs. Hudson used to be a demon hunter."

Mason smiled. "Crazier than you being Famine?"

Francine chuckled. "Point taken."

"Was she the blue-haired lady with you at the cemetery?"

Dang. Of course, the detective had seen the video. Everyone had seen the friggin' video on the news last night.

Francine sighed. "No, the blue-haired lady is Karen Longstreet. She's a current demon hunter. Laura's husband Edward was also a demon hunter back in the day, and he started calling old associates for help. Karen drove here and stopped by the cemetery first. She ran into some other recently risen folks and was escorting them back to her car when she saw that the vigilantes had pointed guns at me, Mrs. Hudson, and Rose Dorchester."

"And Rose is?" Mason prompted.

"Come on, Detective." Francine cocked her head. "Surely, you've kissed the cherub watching over her grave for luck?"

A wry smile crossed his face. "I plead the Fifth on that one, Ms. Coy-Astin. How do you know the Eastwood brothers?"

"I don't really." Francine shrugged again. "I learned Hank's first name because someone called him that at the cemetery. Ironically, he thought he was protecting Laura and me by stopping us from driving into the cemetery. I didn't learn his brother's name until today, but I recognized Billy and his truck from last night. He stood in the bed and was spotting for the vigilantes with a pair of binoculars."

"Starting from your meeting with Chief Wright, what happened today?"

Francine spilled out the story of everything that happened, including her inhalation of several dozen Long Johns and what the demon possessing Hank Eastwood had done to the elderly woman's soul.

When she finished, she swiped away the tears of guilt that had trickled down her cheeks. "Is she really Officer Pence's grandmother?"

Mason nodded. "Officer Simmons verified it. She passed away last March."

Francine shook her head. "It's bad enough to lose someone you love. But it truly sucks to lose someone you love twice."

"That's all the questions I have for the moment," Mason said. "Let me speak with Ms. Elante, then you should be able to leave."

Francine stood at the same time as he did, but something else's bothered her. "You do know none of this was Hank Eastwood's fault. There's no way he could have stopped the demon from using him to kill Officer Pence's grandmother."

"All I'm doing is collecting the facts for Chief Wright and the mayor. It's not my decision about what happens next, Ms. Coy-Astin." The detective opened the Florida room door and gestured for her to precede him.

Once again, Francine nibbled on her lower lip as she walked back to the living room. She wanted to trust Oakfield's officials would lend their assistance. But after the Vatican's refusal to send anyone besides Karen, it seemed more and more like she and her sisters were on their own in their battle to stop the Apocalypse.

Chapter 33

The second detective allowed the body movers to take the corpse of Pence's grandmother while Detective Mason questioned Dani. It was the closest Francine had ever been to human death, and it bothered her deeply because she hadn't regretted for one instant the demon deaths she was responsible for. Was she becoming the monster Dani's son thought the Four Horsemen were?

Maybe she wasn't psycho yet with the remorse swirling through her. The elderly woman's demise caused even more guilt because the demon used her to try to kill Francine. On the other hand, maybe the demon was right in his taunts. Heck, if Wila had been with them, she wouldn't have hesitated to take out the demon before it harmed the old lady. But Francine wasn't about to bring up her own fears and regrets in front of the police.

Maybe she shouldn't show those fears and regrets to her sisters either. They didn't need her to bring them down.

When Mason finished with Dani, he told the three Soccer Moms they could leave Pence's house, with the caveat that they were not to leave the county. The women all said they understood, but Francine wondered what any of the Oakfield police would do if the Soccer Moms had to go to, say, Rome to browbeat the Pope into lending them more members of the Vatican taskforce.

She had no question Sable and the other horses could gallop across the Atlantic if they needed to do so.

Officer Graham waited until Detective Mason took Pence down the hall to interrogate him before he turned to Francine. "I'm assuming you ladies don't need a ride back to Oakfield."

"No, but we do have a question," Francine said. "What's going to happen to Pence?"

Graham shrugged. "That's up to the chief and the DA on whether charges will be filed against him." He glanced down the hallway. "It depends on whether he cooperates with the detective, and it depends on what really happened before we got here."

"In other words, he'll get cut a lot of slack because of his personal situation because we have no idea if he was possessed between him leaving the high school and our arrival at his house." Sarcasm dripped from Penny's voice.

"I know he's been a shit to you lately even without a demon riding him," Dani said. "But we both freaked out yesterday over dead relatives. Can you really blame him for freaking out over his grandmother? And worse, watching her murdered right in front of him?"

"I suppose not," Penny grumbled.

"I've got guests at my house, waiting for me to come home." Francine reached for the doorknob. "I'll talk to you guys later."

"We're coming, too," Dani said.

"Thanks for everything, Rick!" Penny called out.

Francine found her minivan parked along the berm behind Officer Graham's patrol SUV. Penny's and Dani's minivans lined up behind hers. Well, it was a better place to be than running around the fields as horses.

"Wait, Francine!" Dani jogged up to her.

"What?" She whirled to face her friends.

Who were so much better at killing demons than she was.

"It wasn't your fault." Dani puffed a few times before she added, "We didn't know what the demons wanted with the risen."

"I should have known when they tried to take Laura and Rose last night," Francine snapped.

Penny caught up with them. "How could you? It's not like any of us have precognition."

"That's seeing into the future," Francine shot back. "I'm talking about the jerks telling me up front what they wanted, and I didn't take it seriously. None of us did. And look what happened. Someone didn't just die. Her soul was totally destroyed." She turned and headed for Sable.

Penny grabbed Francine's hand as she started to yank on the door handle. "You're being too hard on yourself. Last night and today's demon crap could have happened to any one of us."

"But it didn't, did it? They went after the easiest pickings."

"That's not true," Dani protested.

"I can't kill a demon unless it's free floating." Francine looked away from her friends. "I wasn't much help before. Now, with the demons able to use the risen dead against us, I'm totally useless."

"If you were useless, we'd still have the five demons you took out last night, running around and causing mayhem!"

"I don't have the time to debate this," Francine snapped.

"Take care of things at home," Penny murmured. "But can we please talk later tonight? We need to update Wila once she gets some sleep, and I don't want to leave out anything. From any of us."

Francine clenched her jaw. She didn't need them to analyze her failures. Her defeats were self-evident to anyone with half a brain.

"Please," Penny whispered. "We need—I need your analytical talents. I know I'm not thinking straight because of Laura's return. And I didn't say thank you for watching out for her. Thank you."

"All right," Francine said through gritted teeth. "I'll call you later today." She held up her free hand when Penny opened her mouth. "After I take care of business at home."

"That's acceptable." Penny smiled and hugged Francine before she headed for Silver.

"And Penny?"

She paused and turned back to Francine.

"Thanks for letting Brittany stay at your house with the rest of the kids."

Penny smiled and nodded before she resumed her stride to her own minivan.

Dani walked past Francine with a worried expression marring her pretty face, but she didn't say a dang word.

Screw her. Francine jerked open the driver's side door and climbed into the seat. Her stomach rumbled loudly. She pressed the ignition button and glanced at the clock on the dashboard. If she hurried, she might be able to get some more Long Johns before The Bake Shoppe ran out for the day.

Francine pulled into her garage shortly after noon. She'd already devoured a dozen Long Johns between the bakery and her house. Luckily, she had two more boxes to bring inside. It was rude not to have something for her guests, but it was too bad all The Bake Shoppe had left were vanilla-frosted Long Johns.

Sable had been unusually quiet on the way home.

Francine patted the dashboard. "I'm sorry, baby. I don't mean to take my bad mood out on you."

The minivan gave no indication she heard Francine.

It didn't matter. So, her horse thought she was a failure, too, for allowing Pence's grandmother to die. Why deny the truth?

Francine sniffed back the threatening tears, hit the button to close the garage door, and entered the kitchen with the doughnuts.

And blinked in surprise.

"Hey, Miz Francine!" Kirby said from the counter where he was chopping vegetables.

"You got home in time!" Neal crossed the kitchen to give her a kiss before he returned to his wok. He was stir-frying chicken with teriyaki sauce and ginger from the delicious smells.

The broken tiles on the kitchen floor had been replaced, with spacers between the new tiles for the grout once the tile glue dried. Blue painters tape marked a safe path through the kitchen so the replacement tiles weren't disturbed.

Sherlyn sat on a stool at the breakfast bar. She had a small tube of super glue and was painstakingly piecing together Francine's jack o'lantern cookie jar.

"It's almost done." Sherlyn smiled at Francine.

"You didn't have to fix that," Francine protested. She sat the doughnuts on the other end of the counter.

"It gave me something to concentrate on this morning besides the chemo nausea." Sherlyn smiled as she capped the glue tube.

Francine stepped closer and hugged Sherlyn. "Have dinner with us every night, or we can bring dinner over to you on the nights you don't feel like company."

"Mister Neal's teaching me and Korbin to cook," Kirby volunteered.

"Yeah, something besides mac and cheese and processed chicken patties," Sherlyn teased.

Kirby handed the cutting board to Neal, who scooped the mushrooms and vegetables the teen had diced into the wok. The fresh produce sizzled as it hit the hot pan and oil. Neal dumped in a bag of frozen peas and stirred in his homemade sauce.

Korbin entered the kitchen and announced, "The TV trays are all set up."

Francine turned to Neal. "TV trays? We have company."

"And it'll be a little more relaxing for everyone if we're not worried about manners," he said.

"But Rose and Laura—"

"Rose and Laura what?"

Francine turned to find Laura standing in the doorway to the family room. She stared at Francine with her hands on her hips.

"Would appreciate better manners," Francine finished.

Laura laughed. "Sweetheart, I burned bras and smoked pot long before you were born. And my own mother served many a frozen TV dinner on a tray because she and my dad worked full-time at the family locksmith shop. As for Rose, she's still a child. And children are very adaptable."

"All right." Francine held up her hands. "My apologies for insinuating you were old."

"Thank you." Laura turned toward the dented refrigerator and grabbed a couple of six packs of seltzer water before she started giggling.

"What's so funny?" Sherlyn asked.

"I'll tell you how to take out demons with a bottle of seltzer water over lunch." Laura sauntered out of the kitchen with a cat-that-ate-the-canary grin on her face.

The adults sat on the overstuffed chairs or couches with their bowls on the wooden TV trays. Rose chose to sit on the floor around the coffee table with the older boys.

With a mix of curiosity and disgust, she poked at the food in her dish. "What is this?"

"It's teriyaki chicken and vegetables with rice," Neal said.

"Papa says only Chinamen eat rice." The girl frowned at the dish.

"The United States is a mix of a lot of countries these days," Korbin said. "Our food tends to reflect that. Like I love bratwurst and sauerkraut, but none of my ancestors are from Germany."

"I like black-eyed peas," Rose whispered. "But Papa says only ignorant Southerners eat those, but our cook Miz Heddie always saves some for me."

Francine swallowed a groan. This was going to turn into a major education session on race and culture, and she really didn't have time for that. She cleared her throat and looked at Jermaine. "Did Karen and Laura answer your questions about what happened last night?"

"Everything except for one or two," he said. "How are you and your Horsemen friends planning on stopping the Apocalypse?"

Of course, he wanted a definite answer.

"Soccer Moms," Neal said.

"What?" Jermaine said.

"To answer your original question, Jermaine, we don't know at this point," Francine said. "It's only our third week of being the Soccer Moms of the Apocalypse. We're still learning the ropes."

Sherlyn and Mr. Treeger giggled.

"What if we let it happen?" Jermaine said softly.

"Honey! You don't mean that!" Sherlyn looked aghast at her husband.

"Wouldn't it be better to go straight to Heaven and not fight the cancer?" Jermaine looked at his wife so earnestly it made tears well in Francine's eyes.

"There's no guarantee I'll go to Heaven." Sherlyn cupped Jermaine's face.

"Of course you will. You're the sweetest—"

She laid a finger on his lips. "Only God judges, honey. Not you or me. Not even Francine and her Soccer Moms. I've got a lot to fight for. You. Our sons. Our future. Don't give up yet. That's how those demons got inside us. Because we were all giving up."

"All right." Jermaine lifted Sherlyn's hand and kissed the back. "I'll keep fighting, too."

"We will, too." Kirby said while Korbin nodded.

"And I can run errands for you during the day and help clean your house while Francine rides off on her stallion and saves the world," Mr. Treeger added.

"Mare," Francine interjected.

"What?" Mr. Treeger cocked his head.

"Sable is a mare," Francine said. "As in she's a girl, not a boy."

"The gender of your horse isn't the important thing." Mr. Treeger made a face. "Taking care of Sherlyn is."

"I can't ask you—" Sherlyn began.

"You're not asking us." Francine smiled to lessen the potential sting of her words. "We're telling you. You're getting our help. Like it or not. Just like we did for Laura three years ago."

Sherlyn looked at Penny's mother-in-law with a surprised expression. "You had cancer?"

"Ovarian," Laura said. "Take the help. Live your life. Don't let regrets cloud your thoughts and feelings."

"You-you died from cancer though, right?"

Laura released a deep breath. "Because I didn't take care of myself. Because I didn't tell my husband and sons until it was too late. Things can be different for you. Things are different for you, Sherlyn. Take advantage of that, and make the most of it."

🔥　💀　🔥

Two hours later, after the neighbors had eaten their dessert doughnuts and all gone home, Laura helped Francine gather dishes, load the dishwasher, and clean the counters.

"Why'd you lie to Penny about not remembering the last few months of your life?" Francine asked.

"Same reason I told Sherlyn the truth." Laura wiped her hands and hung up her dish towel. "Your neighbor needs hope. The doctors caught her cancer early enough she has a fighting chance to beat it. I waited too long, and I nearly destroyed my family by pretending nothing was wrong the first time around. I drove Ed right into the arms of that cow Deborah Gibson's arms."

Francine froze. "What?"

"Please don't tell Penny or the boys. It would destroy their image of Ed, and I couldn't bear that." A sad smile filled Laura's face. "I'm sorry for dumping on you, but you're the closest thing I've ever had to a girlfriend since my Vatican days."

For some reason, her words struck a chord. Francine knew all too well what it was like not having friends she could trust. It was amazing Penny, Wila, and Dani put up with her over the last several years. And she hadn't been very fair to them this morning.

"Laura, you can talk to me about anything at any time." Francine threw her arms around the older woman. "Thank you for trusting me."

For the first time in the last three weeks, Francine felt like there was enough love and hope in the world to save it.

Chapter 34

Francine called Penny a little before five p.m. "I've got some time."

"I've got a couple of lasagnas in the oven. Would you and Neal like to come over?"

"Do you want me to bring the rest of my houseguests?" Francine said pointedly. "I can't leave them here unprotected."

"I wish I could say yes without it turning into a knock-down, drag-out fight here." Penny sighed. "Gene regrets sending his mom to your place."

"We can do a conference call," Francine offered.

"Screw Edward and his pansy-ass crap," Penny muttered. "Bring them all over."

Relief filled Francine. It would kill her if the demons destroyed another soul because she couldn't stop them.

With the Hudson house full to the gills, the four Soccer Moms retreated to the stone patio after dinner with hot cups of their favorite coffees. Wila laid out kindling and logs in the fire pit, and she soon had a cheery blaze going.

Penny and Francine told Wila about their little talk with Mayor Oldham and Police Chief Wright. When Dani added her two cents, Francine pulled the cash out of her pocket and handed it over for the Long Johns. Wila added the gossip from Oakfield emergency services. At least two first responders had ended up in the hospital psych ward after encountering dead relatives.

"At least, now, we know why the demons want the resurrected folks," Dani said.

Penny shook her head. "But there isn't any rhyme or reason for who is coming back and when."

"Why does that matter?" Francine frowned.

Firelight reflected off the red strands of Penny's auburn hair. "So far, it's been people young enough to know English, and they're confused as hell. What happens when French traders, Spanish explorers, or all the Native American tribes that have lived in this part of the country come back from the dead?"

"Worse, what happens when the dead outnumber the living?" Dani added.

"Then we'll have a blizzard of white people in Oakfield." Wila snickered into her mug of white chocolate mocha.

Not a blizzard. An image of petals raining from the apple tree in her parents' backyard flitted through Francine's mind.

She didn't realize she'd spoke aloud until Wila rolled her eyes. "The resurrected dead are not apple blossoms, girl."

"No, I mean once a flower drops its petals, you can't put them back." Francine stared at the flames licking the logs in the fire pit. "They may have the color for some time after they shed, but—"

"Once the soul's been popped out of the body, the demons can use it?" Wila cocked her head.

"It would make sense why they can possess the living, but they can't harvest the living's soul power," Penny said. "Maybe they don't have the strength to break the bonds between the body and soul."

"Dani's right," Francine said. "We've got to stop the Apocalypse before the dead outnumber the living. Otherwise, we are screwed."

"There's only the four of us," Dani murmured. "How the hell do we protect the entire world and not get ourselves killed in the process? One demon using one soul nearly killed Francine. All they need is four risen souls, hit us at the same time—"

"Maybe we need to look at this another way." Wila interrupted Dani's morbid train. "What if we go after the demons before they make their next move? Like the saying goes, the best defense is a good offense."

Penny considered Wila's suggestion. "And where do you propose to find the local demons?"

"Like I told Mason during interrogation, fear is catnip to demons." Francine grinned. "The most frightened people I've met so far are the vigilantes with guns, wanting to shoot anything that moves in the Oakfield Cemetery."

"Did you recognize any of the people at the cemetery?" Wila asked.

"You already saw the Eastwoods this morning." Francine shook her head. "They're not going to be in any shape to help us tonight—"

She and Penny locked eyes and said at the same time, "Lucas Manewell."

"Who?" Wila looked at each of them in turn.

"He was volunteering at Saint Michael's." Dani turned to Francine. "Is that why he was calling you Lady Famine at the community center this morning?"

"Yeah, but he was also the only one confronting me who took the whole damn situation seriously and wasn't going all puffy machismo at me."

"Puffy machismo?" Wila roared with laughter. "Girl, we have got to update your vocabulary. Rose is picking up the current vernacular way better than you, and she's got nearly two hundred years on all of us."

"We need to have a talk with Mr. Manewell." Penny rose and doused the fire in the pit. "I think he'll help us if he understands his friends are in danger."

Chapter 35

In Penny's kitchen, the adults had a little euchre match going. Edward had actually sat through dinner with his former wife. While he hadn't been warm or affectionate, he'd been civil, which was a huge improvement. From the shouts and shrieks wafting up the stairwell, the kids had their own tournament going with video games.

When the Soccer Moms announced they were heading down to Saint Michael's, Neal laid his cards face down. "Babe, you do know there's a curfew."

"We'll be riding, not driving, honey." Francine leaned over and kissed him. She wasn't going to say a darn thing about her husband and Gene getting trounced by Edward and Gammy Wilkinson while Laura and Karen waited to take on the winners.

"Maybe you should take Karen and me with you," Laura said.

"No, absolutely not." Penny slashed her hand through the air. "We're not putting the rest of you at risk over an informational meeting."

"Call Deke or Father Perez, and let them know you're on your way to the church," Edward said. "If you don't show, we'll know to send out the cavalry. There's an extra can of paint in the utility room closet. Take it with you."

"We don't need paint," Wila complained.

Gammy looked up at Wila. "Man's got a couple of good points, baby girl. You should listen to him."

She huffed. "Gammy, I'm thirty-eight. I don't need a babysitter."

"Then you can borrow his sense, since you didn't use yours with Deion."

Francine froze, waiting for Wila's explosion over the ex-louse.

"What is that supposed to mean?" Wila's tone could have turned Lake Michigan into one giant ice cube.

"I mean getting married only because you were pregnant."

"Gammy!" Wila shrieked.

"I may be dead, but I can count," Gammy Wilkinson said primly, but there was a wicked gleam in her eyes. Everyone else in kitchen struggled to not laugh or smile.

Finally, Penny shook her head. "Let's get going, ladies. We already have a potential Apocalypse on our hands. We don't need World War III, too."

As they entered the garage, Francine edged closer to Wila. "Don't let your grandmother get under your skin. You're not the only one who got pregnant before their marriage."

Wila paused and stared at her. Penny and Dani turned around and looked at Francine, too. Of course, they'd heard her over the rumble of the garage door opening. Dang super hearing.

"You? Little Miss Perfect?" Wila cocked her head.

"Yes, me. You've never had to deal with a broken condom?"

"But Brittany was born well after you and Neal tied the knot." Penny's confusion spiced her words.

"This was when we were in high school." Francine shrugged. "I lost the baby."

"Oh, girl." Wila pulled her into a tight hug. "I'm so sorry." Penny and Dani threw their arms around her, too.

Francine laughed. "All right. All right. Enough. We've got a man to talk to about his buddies."

They separated, and Francine let Famine out. Sable trotted up to her and whuffed against her neck.

"I'm sorry for taking my bad mood out on you," she whispered to the horse. "You ready to run?"

Sable bobbed her head. Francine moved to her mare's side and stuck her foot in the stirrup. As soon as she was settled in the saddle, Sable galloped after the other three horses and riders.

Despite the darkness this time of year, it was fairly early in the evening when the Soccer Moms arrived at Saint Michael's. The community center lights glowed through the windows. Good. The doors would still be unlocked, and they wouldn't be waking anyone. Even better, Lucas's scarlet and gray pickup still sat in the parking lot.

As soon as Francine dismounted, Sable trotted to a parking spot and transformed back into a minivan. The other three mares followed suit. In silence, and in their street clothes, Francine and her friends headed into the community center.

Not even Wila had a snarky comment.

The smell of fresh paint filled the entryway. Mr. O'Leary waited for them inside the main doors while Father McAvoy instructed Coach Cordero and another man, each on their own ladders, how to draw protection symbols over the windows.

"If it isn't my favorite group of Soccer Moms," the coach called down at them. "Thank you for being the only parents not complaining about the postponement of today's game."

"We're sure Courtney gave you and the other coaches more than enough crap today," Wila said. "We don't believe in piling on in an emergency."

The other man looked down at them. "And thanks for donating the coffee to the church, Ms. Hudson. It was great to see Java's Palace open again."

"You're welcome." Penny knew how to treat her customers right.

Francine frowned at the priest. "Father, I thought protection symbols wouldn't work on public places."

"The community center sits on hallowed ground," the priest said. "Father Perez and I re-consecrated the property the entire complex sits on."

"Is that how the demons got into the church last week?" Penny asked.

"Unfortunately during repair work on the main doors fifty years ago, the fresco holding the protection symbols above them was damaged." He sighed. "Mr. Cordero redid those for me, but since the community center is technically part of both the church and the rectory now, this should work. By the way, thank you for sending the other spiritual leaders to learn how to keep out demons."

"What spiritual leaders?" Penny asked.

"All the Protestant ministers in town, along with Rabbi Goldman, Imam al-Bashir, and High Priestess Willow. Pastor Burns said Francine sent them." Father McAvoy looked askance at her.

She winced. "Sorry for not warning you. He was a little disappointed I went to Father Perez and not him for spiritual guidance when my powers manifested. I totally forgot I suggested he talk to you and Father Perez in this morning's craziness."

"It's all right, my dear." Father McAvoy smiled. "It's understandable given the chaos of the last two days."

"Not to interrupt, Father, but Father Perez is waiting for the ladies in his office," Mr. O'Leary said.

"Go on. Go on." Father McAvoy made shooing motions. "I didn't mean to dominate your time."

They followed Mr. O'Leary to the priest's office. Penny hadn't been joking about the tiny size of the room. Francine bit her lower lip to keep from saying something inappropriate. Hers and Neal's closet was bigger than this.

Lucas Manewell sat in the visitor's chair and rubbed his palms against the denim covering his thighs. If he looked nervous last night or earlier this morning, he was positively terrified now.

"Good evening, ladies." Father Perez rose from his chair. "Can you give us some privacy, Mr. O'Leary?"

The former police chief nodded. "I'll be out in the sanctuary if you need me, Father." He left the office. And left the door open.

It wasn't O'Leary's fault. One of the women would have climb on top of books, sit on Lucas's lap, or leave the room in order to have enough space to close the office door.

Dani leaned back to watch Mr. O'Leary. After a few seconds, she straightened. "Okay, he's out of earshot."

"I-I didn't do anything wrong." Sweat beaded and rolled down Lucas's face despite the relative coolness of the church.

Francine crouched next to his chair, and he leaned away from her. "No, you didn't do anything wrong, Lucas. We're worried about the folks who were with you at the Oakfield Cemetery yesterday."

He glanced from face to face. "I know we threatened Lady Famine, but we didn't know who she was at first. And we didn't actually shoot anybody."

"We know," Penny said. "But your friends are just as scared as you are now, which means they can be possessed by demons. That's what happened to Hank and Billy Eastwood this morning."

Lucas gulped. "Did you save them? Are they all right?"

"They're both going to be in the hospital for a couple of days," Wila said. "A demon can do a serious number on a person's mind, but they will physically recover."

"We need the names, addresses, and phone numbers for the rest of the folks," Francine said. "They're in danger of possession because of their fear, too. That's why we've got to find them."

Lucas stared at his hands resting in his lap.

"Please, Lucas," Francine said. "We need to save them, and we need your help."

"All right," he murmured. "But you've got to promise no one will get arrested."

"As long as it's not your friends breaking the law, they will be fine."

"And if it's the demons doing bad things?"

Francine reached over and patted his hand. "We can tell the difference like we did with the Eastwood brothers this morning. We can tell Chief Wright whether it was the person or the demon possessing them who committed the illegal acts."

Francine just hoped Chief Wright and the Oakfield DA would actually listen to the Soccer Moms of the Apocalypse.

Chapter 36

While Lucas gave Francine the information about his friends, Father Perez scribbled the names, addresses, and phone numbers on a sheet of paper.

"That's a lot of people," Dani commented. "Where do we start?"

"Who's the guy who dropped his gun in the cemetery last night?" Francine asked.

Lucas frowned. "Bill Cooper."

She pushed to her feet. "Let's start with him. He advocated shooting everyone, then left his rifle behind after he saw my alter ego."

"An over-compensator." Penny nodded. "Yeah, we need to check on him first."

"Thank you for your help, Lucas." Francine smiled.

"Please go easy on Bill." He looked up at her with pleading eyes. "He bent over backwards to help me after my car accident. He's a—"

"Good guy," Wila finished. "We know, Lucas. That's who the demons like to go after. Good people in bad situations."

A few minutes later, Francine was astride Sable as she galloped for the west side of the county. Ahead of her, Penny's fur-lined white cape billowed from the speed of their horses. It practically glowed beneath the light of the nearly full moon. Any thought of splitting up in order to cover more people of the list Lucas had given them had been nixed by the other three.

As Wila said, the demons were probably drawn to the Oakfield area by the existence of the Four Soccer Moms. They had no idea how many demons were massing nearby, and they couldn't afford to get picked off one by one. She was being logical, but her statements only reminded Francine of how ineffectual she had been at Pence's house.

Between the speed of their steeds and the fact they didn't need roads, the four of them made good time to the Coopers' property. The two-story farmhouse they approached was built in the late nineteenth or early twentieth century. Wooden clapboard siding was painted Federal Blue with white shutters and trim. Warm light glowed through the sheer curtains on the first floor. An apple orchard stood behind the red barn. It was a lovely, homey place. Why did Bill Cooper feel so insecure?

"Someone's hurt inside," Dani said in her rattling voice.

"A trap?" Penny asked.

"I don't sense any demons nearby," Wila commented.

"They may have already done their damage," Francine muttered. "Sable, take me inside the house."

For the first time today, her mare didn't argue with her. Sable leapt through the wall and manifested in reality long enough for Francine to slide out of her saddle before the horse returned to the yard. The other three pairs did the same. There was no one but the Soccer Moms in the living room.

"This way." Dani took off for the back of the house. Francine and the rest followed into the kitchen.

Wila muttered an oath under her breath at the sight of a bloodied man lying on the linoleum. Francine gasped when Wila rolled him onto his back. Bill Cooper looked like someone had taken a baseball bat to his head and upper body.

Penny stepped back. "I'll call 9-1-1."

Francine crouched on the other side of the injured man. "What do you need us to do?"

"See if you can find some wooden spoons to stabilize his broken right arm." Wila pulled a flashlight from one of the pockets on her fatigues. Bill groaned as she checked his eyes. "Pupils are equal and responsive. That's a good sign, but he may have other injuries."

Behind Wila, Dani grabbed four long wooden spoons from a drawer. She handed them to Francine before she searched through the other drawers.

The man mumbled something even Francine's super hearing couldn't catch.

"Bill, can you hear me?" she said.

"Yeah." He grimaced. "Everything hurts."

"My friend's an off-duty paramedic," Francine said. "She's going to take care of you until the ambulance gets here. Who did this to you, Bill?"

"W-wife, but not." He worked hard to get the words out.

Wila muttered an even more colorful obscenity. "Mr. Cooper, I need to get the fragments of broken teeth out of your mouth before you choke on them."

Dani ripped a couple of dishtowels into strips while Wila swiped Bill's mouth with two fingers. When Wila was done, Dani handed her an intact towel.

"First time, I've never worried about having gloves on hand." Wila shook her head.

Penny return to the kitchen. "Ambulance and an Oakfield patrol car is on its way."

Wila looked up at her with a frown. "Why not the sheriff's department?"

"Apparently, any 9-1-1 calls from us get routed straight to Chief Wright or Detective Mason." Penny laughed. "At least, Wright is keeping his word about backing us up as deputized representatives of Oakfield."

"Where's Emily?" Bill wheezed. "She-she—"

"Is Emily your wife?" Francine held the hand of his unbroken arm, a little surprised her own arms looked human again.

"Yeah, but it-it wasn't her."

"Was it like someone else was inside of her?"

He stared at Francine with fear in his eyes. "Yeah. It-it said it was a demon. That Emily didn't love me anymore and gave herself to it." Tears dribbled down his temples, washing away some of the blood. "Then she, then she grabbed one of our son's baseball bats and started hitting me."

"That's not how possession works," Francine said fiercely. "Was she as afraid about the dead coming back as you are?"

"More." Pain crossed his face as Wila splinted his broken arm. "Our kids are away at college. Emily thinks the world is ending. She's afraid we will never see the boys again."

"We're all parents, too," Francine murmured. "We understand that fear."

"I don't want zombies to eat my kids!" he wailed.

"No one's going to eat your children," she said soothingly. "Did the demon inside your wife tell you where it was going next?"

He started to shake his head, but he stopped himself because of the pain from his grimace. "All it said was its siblings were going to destroy the Four Horsemen of the Apocalypse."

Chapter 37

Francine's sisters resumed their mortal forms before the ambulance and patrol vehicle arrived. They all were a little surprised to see Chief Wright himself climb out of the police SUV. When he came into the Coopers' house, he nodded at Wila.

"Good to know someone responsible is running with this pack, Ardale," he teased.

Francine opened her mouth to say something, but Penny stepped on her foot. Hard. She bit her lip to keep from crying out.

Chief Wright motioned for them to follow him outside while the paramedics checked out Bill Cooper. Under the light of the front porch, he scowled.

"Let me guess. A demon took a baseball bat to this guy."

"Worse," Penny said. "A demon possessed his wife in order to beat the crap out of him with a baseball bat. It's beside the couch, and no, we didn't touch it. But his wife was not responsible for this. It was a demon."

"Any ideas where the wife went?"

"According to Bill, the demon inside Emily said it and the other demons planned to kill us." Francine waved her hand to indicate her and her sisters.

"But that's nothing new," Wila added.

"Give me a sec." The chief pulled out his cell phone, walked over to the pickup parked in next to the house, and took a picture of the license before he returned to the porch. "Let me run the Coopers through my computer.

I'll put a BOLO out for the wife. Keep your fingers crossed the demon didn't abandon the wife's vehicle somewhere."

While he strode back to his SUV, Francine looked at the other Soccer Moms. "Now what? Continue down the list Lucas gave us?"

"How many more situations are we going to find like Bill Cooper?" Dani asked.

"His beating was a delaying tactic," Wila said. "The demons are buying time."

"But buying time for what though?" Penny leaned a hip on the porch railing.

A shudder ran through Francine. "To gather the souls of the recently risen."

"But if Father McAvoy has been advising the other spiritual leaders on how to protect their places of worship—" Penny started.

"To get rid of us, they need the largest collection of resurrected souls available." Panic stabbed Francine's nerves. "The demons' target is the high school."

Chapter 38

Picking up on Francine's anxiety, Sable danced on the gravel drive while Penny called her house to let the spouses and hunters know where they were going this time. Silver stood patiently with Verde and Scarlett.

"Maybe we should go back to your place and have the hunters accompany us," Francine murmured. "We're going to be outnumbered."

"And who's going to watch our children if they do," Dani responded. "We got to pull up our big girl panties and deal with these demons."

"That's assuming I'm right, and they show up," Francine muttered.

"They will," Wila said.

All four women had already transformed into their respective Soccer Mom personas. Francine mounted Sable. She leaned forward and patted her horse's neck. "Back to the high school as fast as you can. We need to beat the demons there."

Chief Wright jumped out of his SUV. "Wait! Where are you going?"

"We think the demons are going to strike at the high school," Penny shouted. "It's the only unprotected place in town with a large contingent of the resurrected."

She and Silver took the lead, and the four horses galloped into the night, their riders bent low over their saddles.

Lights were on inside and outside the gymnasium. There were fewer cars in the teachers' parking lot. Everything seemed peaceful and quiet as the Soccer Moms rode onto the high school property until they heard the first muffled scream from inside the building.

Their steeds phased through the walls into a melee of panicked people in the gymnasium. A civilian woman and a handful of living police officers were possessed, and the demons were firing randomly into the crowd. No, not randomly. They were only shooting to injure the resurrected.

"They're here!" one of the demons shouted. At the cue, black smoke poured from the gym's vents. Puffs split off from the main body and targeted the living Red Cross volunteers who were desperately trying to evacuate their charges.

"We'll take the possessed," Penny shouted. "Get the resurrected out of here, Francine."

Of course. She wasn't any damn help in a fight.

She slipped from Sable's back. "This way!" She picked up a couple of the small children and led the way out of the gym. Thankfully, the risen people followed her, assisting the injured out of the war zone as they went.

Francine kicked the security gate that separated the public areas from the classrooms. The locked snapped, and the crowd with her surged past her. Behind them, the black smoke came after the resurrected. She thrust the two children into the arms of the couple in Red Cross shirts bringing up the rear.

Manifesting her scales, Francine swung at the black smoke. White light flashed and howls of pain roared from the demons. But there was no way to hold them all back.

Unless . . .

The damn demons needed a living human to possess. Well then, she'd give them an irresistible target.

She stood in the middle of the hallway, her arms spread wide. She thought of every terrible thing in her life and the lives of those she loved. The way Courtney Lasser treated Francine and Brittany because her daughter was a better player than Courtney's son. The unfairness of Sherlyn having cancer just as Kirby was about to graduate. Poor Justine's own battle with leukemia, and Laura succumbing to her ovarian cancer. Francine's uncle molesting her. Her failure as a Soccer Mom of the Apocalypse.

As she suspected, all that pain and suffering was catnip to demons. They entered her, thousands of them, tried to possess her.

But she had a tight grip on each and every one of them. A pit opened up before her, and she jumped into it.

She knew she was dying and there wasn't a damn thing she could do to stop it without letting go of the demons. And that, she could not do. She couldn't let another innocent die.

She just couldn't live with herself if she did.

Chapter 39

Francine was being crushed under a mound of demons. She couldn't move. Not even a pinkie.

Fine. She'd take them all to Hell with her.

"No, Francine, don't do it." The voice sounded familiar. Very familiar.

A glowing hand reached between the demon bodies. "Come with me."

"Coach Cordero?"

"That's one of my many names." He chuckled. "Please, Francine. Take my hand. I can't afford to lose one of my generals before the battle that is to come."

"If you are who I think you are, then you should know we're not going to let the world be destroyed."

"That's not your job. The Horsemen are supposed to stop the Apocalypse and save humanity."

That wasn't what the various versions of the Bible had said. But after so many translations into so many languages, did she know that for sure? Or was it merely what she wanted to believe?

"Are you lying to me?" she demanded. It was getting harder to breathe. Even with their ethereal forms, the press of demons on top of her was crushing her heart and lungs.

"No, Francine, but it's your faith that will make the difference. Either you have faith in me, or you don't. Either you have faith in yourself, or you don't. You're human, which means you have the free will. You choose whether you have faith."

"Even with these powers?"

"Even with the abilities of Famine at your command."

"Why didn't you tell us?"

"You had to choose to take the mantle of a Horseman. I could not force you."

"Didn't feel like it to us," she grumbled.

"Are you coming with me?"

"Wait. What about all these demons?"

"Take my hand, and they will fall. You'll no longer be there to hold them out of the pit."

Francine grabbed the glowing hand. The essences of the demons fell past her, screaming and shrieking when they couldn't touch her anymore or hold onto the edges.

She blinked. A man's head silhouetted by a yellow-white halo appeared above her. Then, everything went blank.

Chapter 40

The whistle of air forcing its way up her nose irritated her. Francine swatted at it, but the whistle only changed pitch.

"No, dear, no. It's an oxygen tube. You're in the hospital." A woman's voice. English accent.

Francine opened her eyes. A no-nonsense woman stood by her bed in a gray sweater and black slacks. A black headband held back her gray bob.

"What am I doing at the hospital?"

"Holy crap, you're awake!" Karen shouted at the top of her lungs. Or that's what it seemed like to Francine before the demon hunter dashed back out of the hospital room.

The gray and black woman clucked her tongue. "The American hunters can be so excitable."

"Who-who are you?" Francine forced out. Good grief her voice sounded worse than when she wore Famine.

"Sister Joan." The woman chuckled. "Or I was a nun before I died. I'm not sure if my vows count after I'm resurrected. Before you ask the next question, it's Sunday morning."

"You're part of the Vatican taskforce, aren't you?"

"Again, I was. A long time ago."

"Why am I here?" Francine asked again.

"You overextended yourself taking on a thousand demons by yourself, my dear." Sister Joan reached over the bed railing and patted Francine's arm. "You were dehydrated and malnourished, nothing but skin and bones when your sisters found you. The rest of us weren't sure you would make it through the night, but your sisters were. They said you were the strongest out of the four Soccer Moms."

No, she wasn't, but Francine didn't have the strength to argue with the resurrected nun. "Why are you here? Last I knew, the Vatican refused to send anyone besides Karen."

Sister Joan made a face. "It took some time, but someone among the cardinals with a lick of sense finally realized they could supplement the living hunters with the resurrected ones."

"That's awesome." Francine swallowed hard. "I think. Where's Coach Cordero?"

"Who?"

Crap. Maybe He didn't want people to know his real identity. That knowledge would definitely cause a riot in town, for sure.

"I'm sorry." Francine cleared her throat. "I think I still have demon gunk in my head. I meant, where's my husband?"

"I'm sure Karen is calling him and the other Soccer Moms right now." Sister Joan laughed. "Soccer Moms, I love it, but you do know the proper term is Football Moms of the Apocalypse, don't you?"

Chapter 41

Three days later, Francine Coy-Astin breathed a little sigh of relief as she examined herself in the full-length mirror in her bedroom. Her panties and bra were still a little loose. Her face had a bit of a gaunt appearance. And blond fuzz covered her head. But she no longer looked like a half-dead starvation victim. Holding that many demons inside herself had taken a severe toll on her human body. No wonder the doctors feared she wouldn't survive.

It was one thing to look like a starvation victim while she channeled Famine. It was another to look like that while she was human.

Neal stepped up behind her and wrapped his arms about her waist. "Glad to see you looking healthy again, babe."

She smiled and luxuriated in the simple joy of his body warmth through the brown buttoned up coat he wore. "I guess I needed to be myself instead of trying to be the perfect wife, the perfect mother, and the perfect Soccer Mom."

"You were already perfect when I met you." He nuzzled her neck.

She turned to face him and ran her hands over his newly shaved head. "Thanks for ditching the toupee."

He grimaced. "I guess we both were pretending to be perfect."

"We wanted a perfect life," she murmured. "The problem is there's no such thing. But what we do have is pretty damn awesome."

"Just don't think you have to be the only one to save the world. You've got me, Brittany, and the rest of the Soccer Moms to watch your back." He kissed her forehead.

She let the power of Famine wash over her. Her black cloak didn't seem as raggedy as before, and her skin didn't feel as weirdly tight. "Shall we, Uncle Fester?"

Neal held out his elbow. "Of course, my queen."

They walked out to the upstairs hallway. Francine yelled, "Girls! You ready to go trick-or-treating?"

Rose rushed out of the guest bedroom first, followed by Justine and Brittany. All three girls wore jeans, flannel shirts, hunting jackets, and boots. On the other hand, Karen wore a tan trench coat over black dress slacks, a white button-down, and a loose black tie.

"Thanks for being Famine tonight, Mom." Brittany grinned. "We are definitely hitting the Lassers' house first!"

Soccer Moms
of the
Apocalypse

War in White Chocolate

On Sunday evening, Wila Ardale sat in the lotus position on the thick, plush carpet of her family room with her eyes closed. Despite the nag champa incense wafting through the air and her yoga pose, she jerked when pots banged in her kitchen. Her role as War, the third Horseman of the Apocalypse, or rather Soccer Mom of the Apocalypse as her friends preferred to call themselves, seemed to feed on her PTSD. The same PTSD she believed she had mostly dealt with after she left the army nearly fifteen years ago.

Her right eye opened and peered up at Grandpapa's antique clock on the stone mantel above the fireplace. Five frickin' minutes. It had been five frickin' minutes and she couldn't even get into the first level of a meditative trance. Not with her grandmother rattling around in the kitchen.

Her recently risen from the dead Gammy.

Wila knew Gammy had dealt with her own stress by cooking when she was alive. Apparently, it held true in her resurrection. But the damn noise was driving Wila crazy. She was used to total silence on her days off work while Derek was at school or at his father's house like right now.

And the ex-louse would be bringing her son home at any moment. She trusted Derek to remain silent about Gammy living with them, and the ex-louse usually went out of his way to avoid talking to Wila. He would drop Derek off at the door as usual, and she wouldn't have the faintest chance of dealing with him for two whole weeks. So, why was she worried about Deion finding out about Gammy?

"Me-arow," Malcolm complained at another bang. Wila looked over at the couch. Her seal-point Siamese sat on his haunches on the middle cushion, cocked his head, and repeated his complaint. His blue-point brother Martin lay on the back of the couch and swished his tail in agreement.

"I know, I know," Wila muttered. "I'll go talk to her."

Martin sniffed to indicate he didn't think anything Wila said to Gammy would work. With another round of banging from the kitchen, he had a point.

Wila stretched out for a count of fifteen before she rolled to her feet and padded into the kitchen. Gammy crouched before the open pots and pans cupboard, shuffling things around loudly.

"Whatcha looking for, Gammy?" Wila asked.

"Don't you have a colander, girl?" Gammy straightened.

Wila walked around the breakfast bar. A large bundle of collard greens sat in the sink. Yep, her grandmother was cooking again.

"Gammy, I told you that you don't have to cook every meal for us," Wila said. "And especially not tonight. Derek is eating dinner with—" It took all her will not to refer to Deion as the ex-louse in front of her grandmother. "—with his dad tonight."

Gammy shook her head sadly. "I can't believe you and Deion are divorced. I remember you two being so happy that day your blessed little baby was born."

"Well, that was before I found out he was screwing my best friend Rashida, our babysitter Kristy, and his secretary Eileen," Wila grumbled.

"Eileen?" Gammy's forehead wrinkled. "She's your mama's age, and she's white."

Wila crossed her arms and leaned her left hip against the counter. "Tell me something I don't know."

"Still need a colander for the greens." Gammy waved at the leafy vegetables in the sink.

"I can throw in a pizza from the freezer for dinner." Wila stalked over to her refrigerator. "That's plenty for the two of us."

"That processed food isn't good for you," Gammy lectured.

Wila took a deep breath before she turned to face her grandmother. "I can pick up soup, salad, and sandwiches from the café down the street. That would be healthier, right?"

Gammy shook her finger at Wila. "It's a waste of money eating out all the time. How are you going to save up Derek's education by spending willy-nilly?"

"The money for Derek's education is already set aside." That had been the one thing she refused to compromise on during the divorce negotiations. Fortunately, the ex-louse didn't want to ruin his reputation in front of the family court judge.

"Fine, but that doesn't take care of these collard greens, baby girl. And I bought a nice ham hock, too."

Wila tensed at the reminder her friend Francine was doing more for Gammy than she was. Like buying Gammy clothes and taking her grocery shopping while Wila was at work. She didn't need a white savior to take care of her own damn family.

Guilt niggled at her. That wasn't fair to Francine. She made the same efforts for Wila as she did for Penny and Dani. It's just that Francine had blossomed as a Soccer Mom while Wila . . .

She was barely keeping her shit together.

Swallowing the raging anxiety, Wila pointed out, "I have a strainer I use for pasta."

"Too small." Of course, the old woman wanted a bigger colander. She was used to cooking for her eight children, their significant others, her grandchildren, and all the cousins. However, Mom and most of the aunts and uncles had passed. Dad lived in Florida with his girlfriend. And all the cousins had scattered across the fifty states to wherever their jobs took them. Just another reminder of how alone she was, except for Derek.

And Gammy.

"How about we go shopping in the morning?" Wila said. "We'll find you a colander you like, and I'll help you with cleaning greens before I head into work. Then I'll be out of your hair and you can cook to your heart's desire."

Gammy stared into Wila's eyes before she rested a warm callused palm against Wila's cheek. "You always were a good girl, Wila."

Her eyes burned, and she laid her own hand over Gammy's. "You have no idea how much I've missed you."

Gammy laughed. "I admit I never thought the sounding of the trumpets on Judgement Day was going to be like this."

"Those sounding trumpets are what we're trying to avoid, Gammy," Wila said sternly. Because she couldn't think of failure. Not stopping the Apocalypse meant her son would never have the life he deserved.

The security system beeped, and Derek shouted, "Mom, I'm home!"

Speak of the devil.

"In the kitchen!" she responded.

He raced in, skidding on the hardwood, and hissed, "Dad's here."

His warning was too late to rush Gammy upstairs to her bedroom. Sure enough, the ex-louse walked in behind Derek. His confident swagger had first attracted Wila to him, but now, it just pissed her off.

She crossed her arms. "What do you want, Deion? None of your girl-friends are here."

"Ah, Wila, always a pleasure to speak with you." His equally confident smile faltered when he noticed who was standing beside her. "Gammy La-tricia? B-but you're dead!"

"You got no right to address me with any familiarity, Deion Jackson." Gammy shook her index finger at him. "If my great-grandson weren't standing right here, I'd be giving you a piece of my mind."

"What is she doing here?" Deion spluttered.

Wila glared at him. "It's been three weeks since the dead started rising from their graves. You may not have a lick of compassion, but I'm not about to turn my grandmother away from my home."

Something alien shone from Deion's eyes, but this was normal human malice. He wasn't possessed by a demon, as much as she wanted to blame her ex's attitude on someone, or something, else.

"Derek, get in my car," he demanded.

"What? No!" Derek protested. "I'll see you Wednesday after school. Like always."

"You had your weekend with him, Deion," Wila said. "You've delivered him safely home. It's time for you to go."

Deion said nothing. None of his usual attempts to intimidate her or threaten her with legal action. Nor did he reprimand Derek for giving him lip. No, Deion pivoted and stalked out of her kitchen. She followed to make sure he exited her house, and she watched him back out of her driveway.

His silence indicated he planned something. Something she wasn't going to like.

Too bad her flaming sword didn't work on living ex-husbands.

Acknowledgements

Much gratitude and respect go to Elaina Lee of For the Muse Design for the Soccer Moms covers and JW Manus for the internal formatting. Their professionalism and dedication to their respective crafts make my stories look their best.

A special thanks go to the crew at Dragonsteel Entertainment for showcasing the Soccer Moms of the Apocalypse in their YouTube video and encouraging a lot of new-to-me readers to check out my books.

And most of all, much love to my Darling Husband, Genius Kid, and Princess Bella. You keep me sane when I'm on a deadline.

Suzan Harden transitioned from writing information technology manuals for companies and legal articles for a law enforcement magazine to her first love, fantasy and science fiction in all their forms. She's the author of the Bloodlines, the 888-555-HERO, and the Justice series.